Adèle G

The Green Behind the Glass

Love Stories

LIONS · TEEN TRACKS

First published in Great Britain 1982
by Hamish Hamilton Children's Books
First published in Lions Teen Tracks 1984
This impression 1989

Lions Teen Tracks is an imprint of
the Children's Division, part of
the Collins Publishing Group,
8 Grafton Street, London W1X 3LA

Printed and bound in Great Britain by
William Collins Sons & Co. Ltd, Glasgow

Acknowledgements

'You Make Me Feel So Young' from the film *Three
Little Girls in Blue*. Music by Josef Myrow; words by
Mack Gordon © 1946 20th Century Music Corp.
Original publishers Brigman, Vocco and Conn Inc.
British publishers Chappell Music Ltd.

Contents

For Laura

1. *The Green Behind the Glass*

The telegram was addressed to Enid. Sarah put it carefully on the table in the hall. The white envelope turned red in the light that fell through the coloured squares of glass above the front door. She had no desire to open it. She knew that Philip was dead. The possibility that he might be wounded, missing, captured, never occurred to her. It was death she had been expecting, after all. These were only the official words setting it out in writing. For a moment, Sarah wondered about the people whose work it was every day to compose such messages. Perhaps they grew used to it. The telegraph boy, though, couldn't meet her eyes.

"Telegram for Miss Enid Hurst," he'd said.

"I'll take it. I'm her sister. They're all out."

"Much obliged, I'm sure." He had thrust the envelope into her hand and run towards the gate without looking back, his boots clattering on the pavement. The envelope had fluttered suddenly in a rush of wind.

Sarah sat on the oak settle in the hall and wondered whether to take the message to Enid in the shop. To them, she thought, to the writers of this telegram, Philip is Enid's young man. He was. Was. Haven't we been embroidering and stitching and preparing for the wedding since before the War? Enid will enjoy mourning, thought Sarah. It will become her. She will look elegant in black, and she'll cry delicately so as not to mar the whiteness of her skin, and dab her nose with a lace-edged handkerchief, and wear Mother's jet brooch, and all the customers will sigh and say how sad it is, and young men will want to comfort and console her, and

1

they will, oh yes, because she didn't really love him.

"She didn't really love him," Sarah shouted aloud in the empty house, and blushed as if there were a part of Enid lurking somewhere that could overhear her. "Not really," she whispered. "Not like I did." I know, she thought, because she told me.

Enid is sewing. I ask her: "Do you really love him, Enid? Does your heart beat so loudly sometimes that you feel the whole world can hear it? Can you bear it, the thought of him going away? Do you see him in your dreams?"

"Silly goose, you're just a child." She smiles at me. She is grown-up. Her face is calm. Pale. "And you've been reading too many novels. I respect him. I admire him. I am very fond of him. He is a steady young man. And besides, ladies in real life don't feel those things, you know. It wouldn't be right."

But I felt them, thought Sarah. And other feelings, too, which made me blush. I turned away, I remember, so that Enid should not see my face, and thought of his arms holding me, and his hands in my hair and his mouth . . . oh, such a melting, a melting in my stomach. I loved him. I can never say anything. I shall only be able to weep for him at night, after Enid has fallen asleep. And I shall have to look at that photograph that isn't him at all, just a soldier in uniform, sepia, like all the soldiers. Enid will keep it there between our beds. Perhaps she will put it in a black frame, but after a while, I shall be the only one who really sees it.

Sarah tried to cry and no tears would come. It seemed to her that her heart had been crushed in metal hands, icy cold and shining. How could she bear the tight pain of those hands? But soon, yes, she would have to take the telegram and walk to the shop and watch Enid fainting and Mother rustling out from behind the counter. Mrs. Feathers would be there. She was always there, and she would tell, as she had told so often before, the remarkable story of her Jimmy, who'd been posted as dead last December and who, six months later, had simply walked into the house, bold as you please, and asked for a cup of tea.

"You're mine now," Sarah said aloud to the telegram, and giggled. Maybe I'm going mad, she thought. Isn't talking to yourself the first sign? I don't care. I don't care if I am mad. I shall go and change into my blue dress, just for a little while. Later, I shall have to wear dark colours, Philip, even though I promised you I wouldn't. Mother will make me wear them. What will the neighbours say, otherwise?

"Philip is like a son to me," Mother used to say, long before he proposed to Enid. "One of the family." Perhaps that is why he proposed. Or perhaps Mother arranged the whole thing. She is so good at arranging. Enid is piqued, sometimes, by the attention Philip pays to me. I am scarcely more than a child. Mother says: "But of course, he loves Sarah, too. Isn't she like a little sister to him?" When she says this, I clench my fists until the nails cut into my palms. I don't want that kind of love, no, not that kind at all.

Sarah laid the blue dress on the bed, and began to take off her pinafore. The sun shone steadily outside, but the leaves had gone. Swiftly, she pulled the hat box from under the bed, and lifted out her straw hat with the red satin ribbons. It was a hat for long days of blue sky, green trees and roses. I can't wear it in November, she thought. It had been wrapped in tissue paper, like a treasure. Sarah had looked at it often, remembering the afternoon in Kew Gardens, so long ago, a whole three months. She had thought of it as the happiest day of her life, a day with only a small shadow upon it, an insignificant wisp of fear, nothing to disturb the joy. But now Philip was dead, and that short-lived moment of terror spread through her beautiful memories like ink stirred into clear water.

Enid's sewing-basket was on the chest of drawers. Sarah

was seized suddenly with rage at Philip for dying, for leaving her behind in the world. She took the dress-making scissors out of the basket, and cut and cut into the brim of the hat until it hung in strips, like a fringe. The ribbons she laid beside her on the bed and she crushed the crown in her hands until the sharp pieces of broken straw pricked her, hurt her. Then she snipped the long, long strips of satin into tiny squares. They glittered on her counterpane like drops of blood. When she had finished, her whole body throbbed, ached, was raw, as if she had been cutting up small pieces of herself. She lay back on the bed, breathless. I must go to the shop, she told herself. In a little while. If I close my eyes, I can see him. I can hear his voice. And Enid's voice. Her voice was so bossy, that day:

"You can't wear that hat," Enid says. "It's too grown-up."

"I am grown-up." I dance round the kitchen table, twirling the hat on my hand, so that the ribbons fly out behind it. "I shall be seventeen at Christmas, and it's just the hat for Kew."

"I don't know why you're coming, anyway," says Enid.

"She's coming because it's a lovely day, and because I invited her," Philip says.

He is leaning against the door, smiling at me.

"Thank you, kind sir." I sweep him a curtsey.

"A pleasure, fair lady," he answers, and bows gracefully.

"When will you two stop clowning?" Enid is vexed. "You spoil her all the time. I've had my hat on for fully five minutes."

"Then let us go," he says, and offers an arm to Enid and an arm to me.

In the street, Enid frowns: "It's not proper. Walking along arm-in-arm . . . like costermongers."

"Stuff and nonsense," says Philip. "It's very jolly. Why else do you suppose we have two arms?" I laugh.

4

Enid wrinkles her nose.

"August is a silly time to come here." There is complaint in Enid's voice. She is sitting on a bench between me and Philip. "The camellias are long since over, and I love them so much. Even the roses are past their best." She shudders. "I do dislike them when all the petals turn brown and flap about in that untidy way."

"Let's go into the Glass House." I jump up and stand in front of them. Enid pretends to droop.

"Philip," she sighs, "you take her. I don't think I could bear to stand in that stifling place ever again, among the drips and smells."

Philip rises reluctantly, touches Enid's shoulder.

"What about you, though," he says. "What will you do?"

"I shall sit here until you return." Enid spreads her skirts a little. "I shall look at all the ladies and enjoy the sunshine."

"We'll be back soon," I say, trying to keep my voice from betraying my excitement. Have I ever before been alone with him? Will I ever be alone with him again? Please, please, please, I say to myself, let the time be slow, don't let it go too quickly.

Philip and I walk in silence. I am afraid to talk, afraid to open my mouth in case all the dammed-up love words that I am feeling flood out of it.

We stand outside the Glass House for a moment, looking in at the dense green leaves pressing against the panes. A cloud passes over the sun, darkens the sky, and we are both reflected in the green. Philip's face and mine, together. In the dark mirror we turn towards each other. I stare at his reflection, because I dare not look at him, and for an instant his face disappears, and the image is of a death's head grinning at me, a white skull: bones with no flesh, black sockets with no eyes. I can feel myself trembling. Quickly, I look at the real Philip. He is there. His skin is brown. He is alive.

"What is it, Sarah? Why are you shaking?"

I try to laugh, and a squeak comes from my lips. How to explain? "I saw something reflected in the glass," I say.

"There's only you and me."

"It was you and me, but you . . . you had turned into a skeleton."

The sun is shining again. Philip's face is sad, shadows are in his eyes as he turns to look. I look too, and the skull has vanished. I let out a breath of relief.

"It's only me, after all," he says.

"But it *was* there. I saw it so clearly. Philip, please don't die."

"I shan't," he says seriously, carefully. "I shan't die. Don't be frightened. It was only a trick of the light."

I believe him because I want to believe him. He takes my hand. "Let's go in," he says.

Inside the Glass House, heat surrounds us like wet felt. Thickly about our heads a velvety, glossy, spiky, tangled jungle sucks moisture from the air. Leaves, fronds, ferns and creepers glisten, wet and hot, and the earth that covers their roots is black, warm. Drops of water trickle down the panes of glass. The smell of growing is everywhere, filling our nostrils with a kind of mist. We walk between the towering plants. There is no one else there at all. A long staircase, wrought-iron painted white, spirals upwards, hides itself in green as it winds into the glass roof. Philip is still holding my hand, and I say nothing. I want him to hold it forever. I want his hand to grow into mine. Why doesn't he speak to me? We always laugh and joke and talk so much that Enid hushes us perpetually, and now he has nothing to say. I think: perhaps he is angry. He wants to sit with Enid in the cool air. He is cross at having to come here when his time with Enid is so short. He is leaving tomorrow, and I have parted them with my selfishness and my love. Tears cloud my eyes. I stumble, nearly falling. My hat drops to

6

the ground. Philip's hand catches me round the waist. I clutch at his arm, and he holds me, and does not let me go when I am upright. We stand, locked together. "Sarah . . ." It is a whisper. "Sarah, I must speak." The hand about my waist pulls me closer. I can feel the fingers spread out now, stroking me. Philip looks away. "I can't marry Enid," he says. "It wouldn't be right."

"Why?" There are other words, but they will not come.

"I can't tell her," he mutters. "I've tried. I can't." He looks at me. "I shall write to her. Soon. It's a cowardly thing to do, but I cannot bear to face her . . . not yet. Not now. Sarah?"

"Yes?" I force myself to look up.

"Sarah, do you know," his voice fades, disappears, ". . . my feelings? For you?"

"Me?" My heart is choking me, beating in my throat.

"I . . . I don't know how to say it." He looks over my head, cannot meet my eyes. He says, roughly: "I've thought it and thought it, and I don't know how to say it." He draws me closer, close to him. I can feel his buttons through my dress. I am going to faint. I am dissolving in the heat, turning into water. His arms are around me, enfolding me. His mouth is on my hair, moving in my hair. Blindly, like a plant in search of light, I turn my face up, and his lips are there, on my lips, and my senses and my nerve ends and my heart and my body, every part of me, all my love, everything is drawn into the sweetness of his mouth.

Later, we stand together, dazed, quivering. I can feel his kiss still, pouring through me.

"Philip, Philip," I bury my head in his jacket. "I love you. I've always loved you." Half hoping he will not hear me. He lifts my face in his fingers.

"And I love you, Sarah. Lovely Sarah, I love you. I don't know how I never said it before. How did I make such a mistake?''

I laugh. Everything is golden now. What has happened, what will happen, Enid, the rest of the world, nothing is important.

''I'm only a child,'' I say smiling, teasing.

''Oh no,'' he says, ''no longer. Not a child.'' He kisses me again, softly. His fingers are in my hair, on my neck, touching and touching me. I have imagined it a thousand times and it was not like this. Wildly, I think of us growing here in this hothouse forever, like two plants curled and twined into one another, stems interlocked, leaves brushing . . . I move away from him.

''We must go back,'' I say.

''Yes.'' He takes my hat from the ground and puts it on my head.

''You must promise me,'' he says, ''never to wear mourning.''

''Mourning?'' What has mourning to do with such happiness?

''If I die . . .''

''You won't die, Philip.'' I am myself again now. ''You said you wouldn't. I love you too much. You'll come back, and we'll love one another forever, and live happily ever after, just like a prince and princess in a fairy tale.''

He laughs. ''Yes, yes we will. We will be happy.''

Walking back together to Enid's bench, we make plans. He will write to me. He will send the letters to Emily, my friend. I shall tell her everything. He will write to Enid. Not at once but quite soon. We can see Enid now. She is waving at us. We wave back.

''Remember that I love you,'' Philip whispers when we are nearly oh. nearly there. I cannot answer. Enid is too close. I sit on the bench beside her, dizzy with loving him.

''You've been away for ages,'' she says. ''I was quite worried.'' His voice is light, full of laughter. ''There's such a lot to look at. A splendid place. You really should have come.''

I am amazéd at him. I dare not open my mouth. Here in the fresh air, I cannot look at Enid. The dreadfulness of what I am doing to her, what I am going to do to her makes me feel ill. But how can I live with my love pushed down inside me forever? Will she forgive us? Will we have to elope? Emigrate? There will be time enough to worry when she finds out, when Philip tells her. Now, my happiness curls through me like a vine. We set off again along the gravel paths. I have to stop myself from skipping. I remember, briefly, the skeleton I saw reflected in the glass, and I laugh out loud at my childish fear. It was only a trick of the light, just as Philip had said. A trick of the light.

There are stone urns near the Temperate House, and curved stone flowers set about their bases. A lady is sitting on a bench in the sunshine under a black silk parasol. The light makes jagged pools of colour in the inky taffeta of her skirts, and her hat is massed with ostrich feathers like funeral plumes. She turns to look at us as we go by, and I see that her face is old: small pink lips lost in a network of wrinkles, eyes still blue, still young under a pale, lined brow. She wears black gloves to cover her hands and I imagine them veined and stiff under the fabric. She smiles at me and I feel a sudden shock, a tremor of fear.

Enid says: ''Forty years out of date at least. Do you think she realises how out of place she looks?''

''Poor old thing,'' says Philip. ''Rather like a pressed flower, all alone in the world.'' He whistles the tune 'Mademoiselle from Armentières.' ''How would you like it?''

''I hope,'' says Enid, ''that if I ever wear mourning, I shall not be so showy. Ostrich feathers, indeed! Mutton dressed as lamb.''

I look back at the old woman, marvelling at Enid and Philip for finding her interesting enough to talk about. I feel pity for her, and a faint amusement, but she does not hold my attention. She is as remote from me, as strange, as if she belonged to another time. I start to run across the grass, as fast as I can. They are chasing me, yes, even Enid, dignity forgotten, is running and running. We stop under a tree, all of us breathless. Philip puts his hands on my waist and twirls me round. I glance fearfully at Enid, but she is smiling at us like an indulgent mother.

We walk home in the dusk. I must leave him alone with Enid at the gate. He kisses me goodbye on the cheek, like a brother, and I go indoors quickly. I am burning in the places where he touched me.

Sarah sat up. Slowly, like a sleepwalker, she gathered up the torn, bruised straw and the scraps of ribbon from the bed and the floor, and put them in the hatbox. When there is time, she thought, I shall burn them in the kitchen fire. She struggled into the blue dress and looked at herself in the mirror. What she saw was the face of a stranger who resembled her: mouth pulled out of shape, skin white, hair without colour. She fastened, carefully, the buttons on her cuffs. Her skin, all the soft surfaces of her body, felt raw, scraped, wounded. I am wounded all over, she thought, and went slowly downstairs. She put the telegram in her pocket, and left the house.

1917 May

"I think James will come to call this afternoon." Enid's fingers made pleats in the lilac skirt she was wearing.

Sarah said: "Do you like him?"

Enid considered the question. The sisters were walking in Kew Gardens. Enid wanted to see the camellias. "Yes," she said at last, "he is a fine man." Sarah thought of James's solid body and long teeth, his black hair and the small brush of his moustache. Over the months, scars had slowly covered the sore places in her mind but sometimes, especially at Kew, the pain took her breath away. She should not, she knew, walk there so often, but she did. She should have avoided the Glass House, but she went there at every opportunity, and stood beside the streaming panes with her eyes closed, willing herself to capture something. Her feelings on that day had been so overpowering, had filled her with such sharp pleasure that always she hoped that their ghosts must still be lingering among the leaves.

Now, she looked at Enid. "I think," she said, "that he will suit you very well."

"He hasn't proposed to me yet," Enid said placidly. "Although I don't think it will be too long. In any case, I shall have to wait at least until November . . ." Her voice trailed away, losing itself among the branches.

"Philip," Sarah said (and the word felt strange in her mouth, an unfamiliar taste, like forgotten fruit), "Philip would be pleased to think you were happy."

"Do you think so, really?" Enid looked relieved. "Of course, I was heartbroken, heartbroken at his death. You remember? I fainted, there and then on the floor of the shop I shall never forget it."

"Neither shall I," said Sarah.

Enid comes out from behind the counter. She says: "What's the matter, Sarah? Are you ill? You look so white. Why are you wearing that thin dress?"

Mother is talking to Mrs. Feathers. It is absorbing talk. I do not think they have seen me.

I say nothing. I give the envelope to Enid. She tears it open: a ragged fumbling of her hands, not like her at all.

"It's Philip," she says. "Philip is dead."

I watch, mesmerized, as she falls in a liquid movement to the ground.

Mother loosens Enid's collar, her waistband, brings out smelling salts. She is weeping noisily. Mrs. Feather says: "I'll put the kettle on for a cup of tea. Plenty of sugar, that's the thing for shock."

I envy my mother every tear she is shedding. I want to cry, and I cannot. The iron grip tightens round my heart.

"His letters," said Enid, "in the months before his death were quite different, you know. Did I ever tell you?"

"No."

"More formal. Veiled. Forever talking about an important matter which he would discuss on his next leave. Not so . . . devoted."

Sarah tried to stop herself from feeling happy at this revelation.

"His last letter was particularly strange," Enid went on. "He was going to tell me something, he said. He couldn't bear to wait another day, but then the letter finished in a scrawl, messy and rushed, because, I suppose, they had to go and capture some hill or bit of wood. I shall never know what it was."

"It doesn't matter now," said Sarah.

"It is vexing, however," Enid said. "I should have liked to know." Part of Sarah longed to tell her, to tell her everything. But she said nothing. They walked on, in the direction of the Temperate House.

"Look," said Sarah. "She's there again. The old lady."

"She looks," said Enid, "as though she hasn't moved since last August. I do believe that is the same dress."

"And the same hat," Sarah added. "Perhaps it's a favourite. It is certainly smart, even though it's black."

"Come this way, Sarah. I don't want to walk past her."

"I do. I want to."

"Then I shall wait for you over there. Truly, I don't understand you sometimes."

I don't understand myself, Sarah thought. Why am I doing this? She began to follow the same path that they had taken before. Almost she could hear Philip whistling . . . Mademoiselle from Armentières . . . hasn't been kissed for forty years . . . hasn't been kissed . . . The air seemed colder. Sarah turned her head away a little as she passed the bench. The lady said: "Such a lovely day, my dear. Don't you think it's a lovely day?"

Under the black feathers, the lady smiled at her, and Sarah

12

could see in her eyes long memories of past happiness, past youth, past love.

"Yes," she said. "Lovely."

"I've seen you here before," the lady said.

"I come quite often. I like it here."

"You had a hat with red ribbons, I remember. I remember many things, and I recall that hat, because I had one once, too, and when I saw you . . ." The lady looked down.

"Yes?"

"You will think it absurd. But there, at my age, I'm permitted to be a little foolish. I thought I was seeing a ghost. A ghost of myself, when I was young."

Sarah smiled, a little nervously. "I must go back to my sister now," she said. "I think your hat is lovely."

The lady smiled, nodded, did not answer.

Sarah walked back to where Enid was waiting. She glanced towards the Temperate House, but the old lady had gone. There was no sign of her anywhere.

Later, on their way home, Sarah and Enid passed by the Glass House. "Are you going in today?" Enid asked.

"No," said Sarah. "I'm only looking in."

She stared at her reflection in the pane dark with the darkness of the green behind it, and touched the veiling that trimmed her hat. At first she did not recognize herself. The veiling looked . . . could it be . . . like feathers? Surely her mouth was not so shrunken, nor her cheeks so white? Her hands seemed stiff, she looked old, she looked wrinkled, she looked — no, no, she couldn't, wouldn't look, like the faded old lady on the bench. A pressed flower, Philip had said. She shook her head, moved it closer to the glass, and the image changed. She was herself again. There was her hat, her own face, still young. She shivered. A trick of the light, that was all it was. Only a trick of the light.

"I don't think," she said to Enid as they walked through the tall wrought-iron gates, "I don't think I shall be coming to Kew ever again."

2. Love Letters

1

"Dearest Pete" or "Pete, dearest" or "Pete, my dearest" or "Pete, my darling" or just "Darling Pete" — which to choose? It was, after all, the first letter and didn't things like how you addressed him have to climb a kind of ladder? Marion decided finally that she'd start with "Dearest Pete" and work up gradually to "Pete, my darling" because that seemed to her to be the most loving, the most tender, the most romantic: the one with the sound of real love echoing round the saying of it when it was spoken.

Down in the kitchen, a radio voice was talking at Dad while he got the tea ready. All Marion's life he had grumbled about being both a father and a mother to her and when she was small she had felt that he was cross with her. Perhaps, she used to think in those days, perhaps it was my fault that Mum died. In the last few years, though, she had realized that Dad enjoyed both the grumbling and the cooking, ironing and cleaning. It gave him pleasure to keep things, as he said, "shipshape and Bristol fashion". Wasn't he one of the best postmen the GPO had ever had? Thirty-five years and no letter ever mislaid or wrongly delivered. I should go down and lay the table, thought Marion. Help him a bit more, but at least it's an easy tea tonight. Steak pies, with baked potatoes and stewed apples. Pies were ten pence off today for staff. There were advantages to working in a supermarket.

Marion looked round her room, waiting for inspiration. What would Sue say if she could walk in here this minute? No pin-ups, just pictures cut from magazines and stuck up on the wall in a kind of patchwork: pictures of lambs and cats and

14

small puppies with ribbons round their necks, country cottages and the tropical beaches that went with advertisements for white rum, whose colours couldn't possibly be real. No sea that Marion had ever set eyes on was that particular shade of transparent, light-filled turquoise. Pete's sea, the sea around the oil-rig, was grey, surely, up there in the cold: metallic and swelling, full of menace, fog drifting over the water, wreaths of mist obscuring the long, iron joints, the hard angles sticking up out of the ice-cold darkness of the waves.

I think of you every minute, Marion wrote. I think of you in the middle of all that black water, and I wish that you could be here with me. Nothing that I do without you seems real, somehow. They all just go past me with their baked beans and their fish fingers and washing powder and chocolate biscuits, and my fingers punch the right figures on the till and I don't see them at all. I see you. When I go to bed at night I think of you, and of all the marvellous fun we had while you were still here. Please write to me whenever you can. I'm just waiting to open a letter and hear your voice from far away when I read it. It's quite cold here, and I expect it's worse where you are . . .

Marion paused. Can I write it, she thought. Can I make the letters that will say it? She blushed and wrote: . . . I wish that I could warm you with my kisses.

Was that too much in the first letter? Was the letter long enough? How to end it? She could picture Pete reading the letter on the end of a hard bed covered with a scratchy red blanket, the kind of bed you might find in a hospital, or in the army. She could imagine what he looked like: dark, slightly wavy hair and blue eyes, the right eyes to look out over the miles of sea all around him. I must finish this letter, she thought. There ought to be some news, but were you allowed to put ordinary news in love letters, or only love, all on its own? She wrote quickly:

15

I quite like the job at the supermarket, really. The manager is fat and jolly. He's called Mr. Barlow, and there's a nice lady called Ena who makes tea for all of us, and a couple of lads behind the butcher's counter who fancy themselves, but don't worry, I'd never even look at someone else when I have you. There's also . . .

Should I? thought Marion, then: why not? Sue wouldn't mind.

. . . a girl called Marion who works with me, and I think we'll get on quite well. I must stop now, because it's nearly teatime, but I'll write again very soon, and please write to me, because I miss you every minute.

All my love and kisses,

Sue.

Marion put the letter in her bag, ready to take to work tomorrow. I hope Sue says it's O.K., she thought. I don't fancy writing it all over again, like homework. I hope Pete likes it too. Marion sat on the bed and stared at the wallpaper (roses — so pretty — she had chosen it herself) without seeing it. She saw Pete. He had blue eyes, she knew, because Sue had told her, and the blue eyes were looking straight at her and they were smiling. It gave Marion a squashy feeling in her stomach.

"Tea's ready," shouted Dad, and the pips for seven o'clock pricked into her mind.

"Coming," Marion shouted back, and walked downstairs, trying to shake away her daydreams before she reached the kitchen. Oh, lucky Sue. Lucky, lucky Sue!

"Dad?" Marion said it without thinking. Her father was busy looking at the *Evening News*, as he did every evening after tea. He put the paper aside.

"Yes, love?"

"Dad, can I ask you something. I just wanted to know . . ." Marion took a deep breath, ". . . d'you reckon anyone'll ever fall in love with me?''

''I reckon they will, our Marion. You look just like your mum, and I fell in love with her, didn't I? You'll be away and married before too long.''

''They're not exactly queuing up at the door, though, are they?''

''You're young yet, love. Only seventeen. Plenty of time for all that. And besides,'' he smiled, ''you're not in the kind of job where you meet a lot of young men. Come and work for the GPO. Falling over lads down there, we are.''

''I might, I suppose.'' Marion looked down. ''But you couldn't say I was pretty, could you? Not honestly.''

Her father thought for a moment. ''Not exactly pretty, no. That isn't what I'd say. I'd say you were wholesome. That's it. Healthy and wholesome.''

Wholesome. Marion considered the word as she washed up. Not pretty. Not attractive. Not sexy. Square and solid, brown hair cut in a fringe, bosom large without being enticing. Healthy. She thought: I feel as if I'm some kind of cake. If Sue were a cake, she'd be layers of feather-light pastry, with jam, and piped curls and flourishes of cream and a sprinkling of chocolate on top. Me, I'm brown and square and wholesome. A date and walnut loaf.

Sue was punching prices on to cans of hot dogs: twenty-three pence, over and over again. Even in her shop overall she looked glamorous, Marion thought. All that leg showing, all that shiny length of pale beige nylon, and those strappy shoes. Mr. Barlow and Ena had had quite a giggle about those.

''Got to stand around a fair bit in this job, lass. Those pretty little feet will be agony come half past four,'' Mr. Barlow's eyes were out on stalks. Sue had smiled, glossy pink lips, smooth make-up, brown eyes like treacle, and said nothing and, as far as Marion knew, her feet never bothered her at all.

Sue came nearer to the till. The shop was quiet now, after the early morning rush.

"Have you got it?" she asked.

"Yes, it's in my bag. You can look and find it."

Sue grinned. "I'll just go and powder my nose, I think. If Berty Barlow comes snooping around, tell him anything that comes into your head."

"I hope it's O.K." said Marion.

"I don't know what I would have done without you," Sue said. "Honestly. I wouldn't know where to begin. I'd just sit there and freeze up. It's really ever so nice of you."

A woman approached the checkout with her trolley.

"Wait till you see it before you say that," Marion whispered, and turned her attention to the till. Sue walked down the aisle towards the restroom. She looked happy.

She hadn't looked happy when Marion had first seen her. She'd been crying: blowing her nose into a lilac-coloured tissue. She was sitting hunched up on one of the two comfortable chairs in the cubby-hole where the staff went for their breaks.

"Hello," said Marion. "I'm Marion. You must be Sue. Mr. Barlow said we'd got someone new starting today."

Sue nodded through her tears.

"Pleased to meet you," she sniffed. "I'm sorry. I mean, I'm sorry I'm like this. I'm not the weepy type normally but . . ."

Marion sat down, embarrassed.

"You can tell me about it. If you want to, that is. Or I'll just go away."

"No, no, please," Sue smiled weakly. "I'd like to tell somebody. I feel so alone."

"I'll make you a coffee, then, shall I?"

"Ta, love, I need one." Sue blew her nose. The tears had dried up a little. She sounded more cheerful. "It's Pete, you see. He's my boyfriend. We've been going together for ages. We're in love." She paused as though she expected Marion to say something. Marion filled the kettle and plugged it in. What was there to say? Sue continued:

18

"He's so . . . I can't explain it. We're like two halves of one thing, do you know what I mean?"

"Yes," said Marion. Well, it wasn't a lie. She'd read about such feelings. She'd seen all those lips on television, glued together in colour and close-up, all that breathing and sighing and staring into one another's eyes. You couldn't avoid it.

"Yes, I know what you mean."

"He's gone," said Sue, drama in her voice.

"Given you up, you mean?" Marion could hardly believe it. Even crying and sniffing, it was clear that Sue was pretty.

"No, it's worse than that." (What could be worse, Marion wondered.) "He's been posted to one of those bloody awful oil-rigs in the North Sea, and he won't be back till Christmas. Can you imagine anything so dreadful?"

Marion could. Christmas was only a few months away, after all, and then he'd be back. She said nothing, to be tactful.

"I miss him. I miss him so much. I feel as if a bit of me had been chopped off. I don't know how I'm going to get through the days. I don't really." Sue took a sip of her coffee, "And as for the nights . . ."

"You could write to him," Marion said quickly. She did not quite feel ready to hear about the nights. To her amazement, this simple remark sent Sue into new floods of tears.

"I'm sorry. What did I say? I didn't mean to make you cry again. What is it?"

"It's the letters. I promised Pete I'd write to him. I swore I would and I can't. I don't know how to begin. I never could string two words together, even at school. I can't even spell properly. I don't know what to do. If I don't write, he'll worry, you see. Think I've gone off with someone else. Oh, Marion, I wish you could help me!"

"Help you with the letter, you mean?" Marion was shocked. Would Sue (she hardly knew her, after all, had

19

only met her a few minutes ago) really let her share the little bubble of love that sealed her and Pete up together and away from the rest of the world?

"I could help you with the spelling, I suppose. I was good at that at school."

"No, I mean," Sue was leaning forward now, anxious, "you could tell me what to say."

"But . . ."

"You've been in love, haven't you? You know what it's like." No, Marion wanted to answer. No, I've never been in love, I don't know anything about it really. Only what I imagine. Only what I dream about at nights. But Sue thinks I have. Sue thinks someone must have loved me as Pete loves her. Maybe they will . . . and if they did, then I'd know what to say. I can't tell her I've never been in love.

"Yes," she said finally, "I could probably tell you what to say. We could work something out together. During our dinner hour maybe."

"I've got an even better idea," Sue smiled. "Why don't you write a letter, and then I'll copy it out and send it."

Marion could hardly find words. Did Sue really mean to hand her love over like an old parcel? Not have any say in it at all?

"What if," she said at last, "what if you don't like what I've written?"

"Then I'll tell you, won't I? And we'll change it, won't we? I must get back to the shop now. They'll think I've disappeared."

"But what about Pete?"

"What about him?"

"Isn't it kind of . . . tricking him? Cheating him?"

"Not really," Sue grinned. "I'm the one that loves him, after all. You've never even seen him. And anyway," she winked, "what the eye doesn't see, the heart doesn't grieve over. See you later, then. Ta ever so much."

"That's O.K.," said Marion, but by then Sue had gone back into the shop.

20

II   September 17th

My darling Sue,

I can't tell you what I felt like when I got your letter
yesterday. I felt as if a little part of you was here with me.
I keep your letter in the top pocket of my shirt, right near
my heart, but I wish I could hold you. I wish it all the
time. All the time I'm working and eating and chatting
to my mates, I just want to feel you next to me, just want
to hold you in my arms and forget about everything else.

Marion said: "Don't you feel funny about it, though?"
She and Sue were arranging cauliflowers into an elegant
pyramid on a shelf covered with plastic grass.

"Don't you feel funny about me reading all the letters he
writes to you?"

"Not really," Sue shrugged. "Can't be helped, can it?"

"But all that stuff, it's sort of private, isn't it? Don't you
feel embarrassed?"

"See worse on telly every night of the week, can't you,
though? And in those fat books you're always reading, with
busty ladies on the cover. I bet there's plenty in those."

"Yes, but that's made up, and this is real. It's different."

"It doesn't worry me, duck, so I shouldn't let it worry
you." She looked at the cauliflower in her hand. "Can we get
this one right on top there, or should I stick it round the back?
It's a bit on the spotty side."

"Round the back," said Marion. Sue seemed to be
behaving quite normally. Marion sighed. If someone had
written a letter like that to her, she would quite probably be
floating high above the assorted pickles and jams at this very
moment on a pink, fluffy cloud, with a thousand invisible
voices murmuring music into her ears.

October 5th

Pete, dearest,

I read in the paper about the gales where you are, and I
wish I could magic you away and into the warm front

room of our house. I love your letters. I love you. I have a special calendar, and I cross off each day when I go to bed, and then I lie there and think of you. I think of you so hard that after a while I can almost feel you kissing me. I dream about you . . .

October 13th

Sue, my beautiful Sue,

I dream about you, too. Every night, and during the day as well. I think about all the things we used to do. Remember the time when we were coming home from Stockport? Remember how we missed the last bus because I was kissing you — we didn't know where we were, or what we were doing, did we? And remember the Christmas dance last year? I'll never forget that. I live it over in my mind all the time. You were so beautiful. I didn't think anyone could be so beautiful. Your skin was like white silk . . .

"Gone a bit overboard this time, hasn't he? Poor old Pete." Sue laughed. "I expect that's all they think about up there, all those lads together."

Marion blushed. "He misses you, that's all. He loves you. I think it's a lovely letter."

Sue wrinkled her nose. "All that bit about skin like silk, though. It isn't as if he'd seen all that much of it, really."

Marion looked away. Sue had never told her. Not exactly, and she didn't want to know, not everything, but now she asked tentatively, trying to match Sue's brisk tone of voice: "What's all this about the Christmas dance, then? Pete seems to think . . ."

"Pete!" Sue laughed. "He's just exaggerating. I tell you, it's the boredom. It makes them all sex-mad. It's a well-known fact. I spilled something all over my blouse, that's all. Just before we went out. And Pete . . . well, I went up to change, and you know . . . Dad and Mum were out, and I let him come up with me while I changed and then, well, there I was in my bra, and we kissed. That's all. Till I put another

22

blouse on. It wasn't anything much. We were late for the dance as it was, so the whole thing only lasted five minutes. He's just made it seem much more important than it was, really."

All morning, Marion could not stop thinking about it. Thinking about hands, Pete's hands on bare skin, his lips touching bare skin. Sue's skin, thought Marion, Sue's skin, so why do I feel as if I'm the one, as if it all happened in my room, as if it had all happened to me?

November 22nd

Pete, my darling,

I bought your Christmas present today and I can't wait to give it to you. I can't believe it. It's only one more month and then we'll be together. I'm so happy. I walk around the shop on air and Berty Barlow says I've got stars in my eyes, and I have and they're shining just for you. I keep your letters tied up with a ribbon, just like they do in stories, because I love them so much. Every time I get one, I feel happy. When I think of seeing you again, I get dizzy. I play a film over and over again in my mind of me meeting you at the airport. I can close my eyes whenever I want to, and just see it: I'll run and run to meet you, and hug you, and hold you close, and we'll kiss and kiss and never stop . . .

December 14th

Sue, my darlingest, lovely Sue,

I can't write much this time because I'm so near to coming home that my hand shakes every time I pick up a pen. I've got a present for you, and something to ask you. Something important. Can you guess?

Marion couldn't sleep. She looked at her watch. Two o'clock. I won't be fit for anything tomorrow, she thought, and it's the Christmas booze-up at the shop. She switched on the light and got out of bed. From the top drawer of her

23

chest-of-drawers she took a pad and went to fetch her biro from the handbag hanging on the back of the door. Then she got back into bed, balanced the pad on her knees and began to write:

Dear Pete,
　　You're coming home tomorrow and I can't bear it. Sue will be so happy, but for me it's like the end of a long dream. All these months while I've been writing these letters for her, I've been putting myself in her place, feeling all the love she feels, remembering things that I never really knew about in the first place. Things like what it feels like to kiss you, the way you talk and smile, and what your hands are like when they hold mine. Now it's all got to stop and it's as though something wonderful is going to end. Those letters from you, it got so I almost believed they were really written to me. I pretended that they were. It made me so happy. I don't even know what you look like and I love you. There it is. I've said it. It's like falling in love with a ghost. Sue showed me those pictures you sent, but they were so small and faraway and you were all wearing those funny oil-rig hats, I couldn't really see you. I've got my own picture in my head and that's good enough. I don't know if you'll come into the shop. I want you to and I don't want you to. I'd like to see you, of course, but also I wish that you could keep on being a lovely dream that I had.
　　　　　　　　　　All my love,

　　　　　　　　　　　　　　　　　Marion.

Marion put the pad on the bedside table and turned out the light. For a while she lay staring at the wall. Then quickly she sat up and fumbled in the darkness and found the sheet on which she had written. She pulled it out of the pad with shaking fingers and tore it across and across again until it was a pile of tiny white flakes all over her bed. Then she buried her head in the pillow and the tears came and came, flowing out of

24

her as if there was to be no end to them, ever.

III

"Marion! Marion . . ." Sue was beckoning her from the till.

"Yes?"

"He's done it."

"What?"

"He's asked me. Pete, I mean. To marry him."

"Oh," Marion forced herself to smile. "That's lovely. Congratulations."

"It's all thanks to you really. Those letters; that's what did it."

"Nonsense. I'm glad I could help. When will it be?"

"Easter, we hope. We're going to have an engagement party. You'll come, won't you? You must meet him. After all, you know him as well as anyone."

"Yes. Thanks. That'd be lovely." Marion turned away and began to pile up assorted biscuits in red and green tins, holly-decked and dotted about with fat robins in honour of Christmas. I can't bear it, she thought. I won't go. I'll be sick. I don't want ever to see him. I can't. I won't. I don't want to. I'll have to buy a new dress. A tiny, half-formed thought rose at the back of Marion's mind. A party. She didn't get asked to many. Perhaps there would be someone there who would make her forget. Perhaps she would see someone across the room. I'll have to go, she thought. Sue'll be ever so hurt if I don't go. And Pete . . . I want to see him. Just the once.

Party voices came floating through the air to Marion, who stood tucked in a corner between the sideboard and the wall.

"Make a lovely bride."

"He's a lucky man."

"Once they're married."

"Only twenty-five quid, and that was on account of knowing Frank who used to work there."

"Shouldn't wonder, but it's different now, isn't it?"

25

"Not real velvet, you see. More the synthetic."

"Another of those?"

"Peanuts?"

"A bit of all right."

Marion sipped her punch and looked down at her new dress. Burgundy, that's what the colour was called. The lady in the shop had said. That sounded lovely, but to Marion it looked, in this light, like what? Old plums? Dried blood? Something awful anyway. What did it matter? This was a stupid, mixed-up kind of party anyhow, with all Sue's elderly relatives and all her friends pushed together into two tiny rooms, with the heating turned full on. Marion had hoped for a disco maybe, or else a smart hotel, but this . . . well, once weddings were in the air, they all came out of the woodwork: aunts and cousins you hadn't seen in years, bringing engagement presents. She tried to imagine what her own party would be like when (if) someone wanted to marry her. Dad and his cronies, and Gran and who else? Ena? Mr. Barlow? Sue? It won't be the same as this anyway because I haven't got a mother. Sue's mother is like Sue, only old. Powder blue jersey dress, and high strappy shoes like the ones Sue wears. Can you inherit your taste in shoes from your mum? Marion looked down at her low-heeled patent leather pumps and sighed. For a moment she had the strong feeling of being at a funeral.

It wasn't the shoes. Not them, nor the dress, nor the old aunts and uncles, nothing like that. It was Pete. Marion searched for him in the crowded room, and found him at last, talking to Sue's dad near the window. He looked, Marion shivered, he looked insignificant. Small (and what was wrong with being small, for heaven's sake? Where had she got the idea that he would tower above her?) with a narrow kind of face, and blue eyes, true enough, but a washed-out shade of blue, and too close together anyway. He had thin lips, hardly any lips at all, really, and when he smiled his mouth made a square, and in that square were lots of other smaller squares of teeth.

"This is Marion," Sue had said.

"I've heard a lot about you," he smiled. "Sue wrote to me. Nice to meet you."

"Nice to meet you, too." Marion whispered and turned away because she couldn't bear to be there when something died, when all the love that she had bottled up inside herself evaporated like liquid left out in the sun.

Later, she tried to be sensible. It's no skin off my nose, she decided finally, after a second glass of punch. He wasn't even mine. Nothing to do with me at all. Why should I care? It's Sue's problem. But how can she love him? She could have anyone she wanted and she chooses him. Well, all right, so he doesn't look like much, but you shouldn't judge by appearances. I mean, who'd come near me, the date and walnut loaf in the dried-blood dress? And yet, I could love someone. I bet there are loads of people I could get on with. I'm all right. Sue likes me . . . lots of people like me . . . when I was helping out at the meat counter the other week, Jim said we should go bowling one night. I don't know that I'd fancy that too much, but he did mention it, that's something.

"Marion?"

"Oh! Hello." It was Pete.

"Your glass is empty. Can I get you another of whatever it was?"

"No, thanks, Pete. I'm a bit tipsy already."

How strange to be talking right to him, and not to feel anything. It's all gone: love, jealousy, longing. It's as if it never happened. In a way, it's a relief, but how empty, how dull the world looks all of a sudden.

"What about something soft, then? A Coke, with lots of ice."

"That'd be nice."

"I'll just go through to the kitchen and get it."

"I might as well come with you. Can I? I'm nearly fainting with the heat in here."

"Sure. Come on."

There was no one in the kitchen.

27

"Let's get some ice," said Pete.

Oh, look at me, thought Marion, look at me, all alone in the kitchen with the man of my dreams. Maybe if I spill Coke all over this dress, I could take it off and he might kiss me, kiss my skin like white silk. Marion giggled.

"I really am a little tipsy," she said.

"This'll sort you out. Here, sit down."

"O.K. It's a bit noisy in there, isn't it?"

"Right. And all those people. Not that I've got anything against Sue's family, mind. No, it's not that . . ."

"There's rather a lot of them, though," said Marion.

"Right. Nice to be able to have a proper chat with someone. Sue thinks a lot of you. She told me. Going to ask you to be her bridesmaid, only don't tell her I told you. She wants to ask you herself."

"Go on," Marion laughed. "Can you see me in cream organza with primroses in my hair? Sue must be joking."

"No, I don't think so," Pete smiled. "You'll look great, don't worry."

Did he really think so, or was he being polite? Either way, one gold star for Pete. He's tactful, anyway.

"She's ever so happy now you're back," said Marion. "She used to long for your letters."

"And I just used to count the days till hers came. I did, honestly."

"I expect they made you feel closer to her somehow."

"They did. That's it exactly. They were marvellous letters, I can tell you that. Terrific, really."

"Well, from what Sue said, your letters were pretty terrific, too."

Pete blushed. Why is he blushing, Marion wondered. And why isn't he saying anything? He's looking all around as if to make sure there's no one here. He's leaning across the table . . .

Pete said: "I'm going to tell you something, Marion, only don't ever tell Sue. I've had it a bit on my conscience, really, for the last few months. You won't tell her, will you?"

28

"No, really. I promise I won't."

"I don't think she'd ever trust me again if she knew."

"What is it?"

He sighed, and looked down at his fingernails. "It's the letters. I never wrote them. Not one. Not even a bit of them."

"Then . . ?"

"Another bloke wrote them for me. I can't string two words together, not really. He wrote them to help me out, like. He's a good chap. Name of Tom Granger. He'd never let on . But it feels funny. Like sharing Sue with another man in a way." Pete shook his head.

"I don't think that's so dreadful," said Marion after a pause. "I mean if he hadn't written them, then Sue wouldn't have got them, would she? And that would have made her miserable."

"D'you think it's all right then? I didn't know what to do when that first letter came. I tried to write but . . . well, then Tom helped me out. But I do love her. The letters don't make any difference to that."

"No, of course they don't. They don't matter a bit. Really."

"I feel better now I've talked to you, though. I feel I've kind of got it off my chest."

"I won't say a word." Marion smiled. "Hadn't we better go back?"

"Yeah, maybe it'll thin out a bit in there, now it's getting late."

One of Sue's uncles gave Marion a lift home.

"Is that you, Marion?" Dad was still awake, then. Waiting up for her. A mother and father to her, all her life.

"Yes, Dad. Only me."

"Had a good party, then?" (The voice cotton-woolly. He'd taken out his false teeth.)

"Smashing."

"Good girl. Sleep tight, then."

"Don't let the bugs bite." She said the words without

29

thinking, just as she had said them almost every night of her life.

In her room, she took off her dress and hung it up carefully. She stroked her own shoulders. Silken skin? Maybe. Maybe someone would think it was. Look at Sue and Pete. Look at Sue, and oh, just look at poor old Pete, and Sue loved him, really did, was going to marry him, wasn't she? You must get a magic lens in front of your eyes when you fall in love, that makes everybody beautiful.

In the dark, lying in bed in the dark, it was safe to think of it. Safe to think. Tom Granger. A new name. An unknown face. What did he look like, and did it matter? For months, she and Tom had written all those letters, poured out all that love. Marion smiled. Tom would probably be lonely up there now that Pete had left. Tom, all alone in the icy fields, furrows of water, leaves of mist clinging to the metal branches of the rig, ice forming on the huge bolts and nails, on all the sharp edges open to the sky. Tom, with his locker full of . . . what? Pin-ups? Books? Cards? Maybe he had someone at home. And then again, maybe not. Maybe he would welcome a friend, a penfriend. That would be a way to begin, as a penfriend. It was worth trying surely? What harm could it do? I've even got the address. I'll never forget that address. Dear Tom, you don't know me, but I'm a friend of Pete's and Sue's, and I wonder whether . . . Marion fell asleep, still smiling.

3. Don't Sing Love Songs . . .

Paris, Thursday, August 10th, 1964

Here we are, then, me and Anna, starving romantically in the next best thing to a garret: a tiny room in a dreadful hotel near the Pantheon. The view from the window is spectacular – wall as far as the eye can see, in every shade of red from brick to sooty maroon. The room itself and all its fixtures and fittings are so filthy as to be almost picturesque. We have both shed our school tunics and are wearing uniform of a different kind: blue jeans, and T-shirts and black PVC macs, which now hang like oil slicks on the back of the door. Nothing else has changed much, though. I still weigh 66 kilos and still have a galaxy of spots around my nose and all over my chin. Thick make-up does little to dim the pink, fiery stars that seem to me to be as large as suns. Anna looks better, there's no denying it. Her long face, with thick eyebrows, is that of a pleasant and ever-so-slightly bored horse, but she also has long legs, and no bottom to speak of, and wears her hair long, straight and black to her shoulders. My hair is cropped very, very short. I'm supposed to look like a sexy urchin but Billy Bunter's more like it. I wear glasses, too. It goes without saying. We are hoping for romance and adventure, and certainly, starving is going to do wonders for my weight.

How do we come to be here?

A flashback. Tuesday, August 8th, 1964, two days ago
''That's Anna from school, Dad,'' I said.
''Nonsense. How could it possibly be?''
''She wrote that she was in the South of France, planning to hitch home. Maybe she's on her way back to England

now.''

"Her parents must be mad. Letting a girl that age hitch-hike all over France on her own.'' That was my mother, of course.

"She was au-pairing.'' Besides, I added to myself, her parents probably think she's safely on a train. That's what she's like at school, misbehaving so languidly and aristo-cratically that by the time anyone notices, it's too late to do anything about it. She is also such a brilliant scholar that teachers usually forgive her. Unfair. They are under the impression that her mind is on higher things. Anna's air of vagueness, of not being quite with you, is one of her greatest assets. What's more, she never blushes. Unlike me. A teacher has only to say: "Now which of you girls did —'' and my spots merge for a time into the scarlet background provided for them by the rest of my face.

The girl was walking on the other side of the pavement. As she came nearer, I could see that it was indeed Anna, and I stood up and yelled her name across the chaotic traffic of August tourists and pushy little French cars. I have a very carrying voice. Anna turned, saw me waving, and began to amble through the line of cars with her nose in the air, look-ing entirely unconcerned about her own and everyone else's safety. French fists were shaken under her chin, brakes screamed, words I wasn't allowed to use hung in the air. Anna smiled pleasantly and said something unrepeatable to the nearest driver. In French. I was impressed. My parents pretended not to hear.

"Gosh, Jill, hello. Hello, Mrs. Simpson. Hello, sir.''

My father beamed. "Sir,'' as Anna knew very well, was the straight way to my father's heart. He jumped up and offered her a chair.

"My dear girl! What a very nice surprise. Do sit down. What'll you have to drink?''

"Oh, heavens, how kind! I don't know, really. May I have a Coca-Cola?''

She sounded as if she had spent her life in a Jane Austen

novel, and had heard the name only yesterday. She also had a habit of calling the United States "The New World".

"Certainly. Garçon!"

She sat down, pushing ill-wrapped parcels into some kind of order under her chair.

We talked for a while, and then my parents, surprisingly tactfully, murmured things about shopping and left me and Anna sitting at the little round table, under the blue umbrella. We arranged to meet them for lunch. Anna sucked her straws, leaned back, and said: "Isn't Paris super? Are you having a marvellous time?"

"Well, you know. Quite nice. Art galleries and bookshops and things. Seeing my uncle Reggie a lot. Nothing special."

My uncle Reggie, my father's brother, lived in a studio on the Boulevard Arago, and was a painter. A real, live one. That was how he made his living — selling paintings of great delicacy and serenity and beauty. Reggie himself was short and dark and muttered into his bushy beard. If you could catch what he said, it was often extremely funny, but hearing him was a problem. His wife, Magda, who worked hard at looking like a gipsy, was a deep-voiced lady who only did the washing up when every bit of crockery and cutlery had been used. This worked out as once every two or three days. It struck me as a sensible arrangement, but my mother was horrified.

Anna said: "I'm thinking of spending a couple of weeks here, enjoying the holidays. My parents have given me an allowance for the next few weeks. I'll have to go and find a room after lunch, I suppose."

"I wish I could come and stay in your hotel with you. It would be like being a student. Or a poet or something."

Anna looked at me. "Why don't you come, then? I haven't much money, and double rooms are cheaper. We'd have a good time."

So, later on, at lunch, we put it to my parents.

"I want to see the room you take," said my mother, but the plan met with little opposition. Perhaps they were as

33

eager to be without me as I was to be without them for a while. The thought had never occurred to me before.

"We'll be here, of course, if you need us," said my father. "You must take the telephone number of the hotel."

"O.K.," I said.

It was arranged that I should have only a very small amount of money for the next couple of weeks. That was the point: to pretend to be poverty-stricken, to see how we would manage.

Later that day, after many interviews with ladies who looked as if they'd come straight from an enthralling hour knitting at the foot of the guillotine, we found our garret. My parents, summoned by telephone, came to inspect. When my mother saw the room, her jaw dropped. She was visibly having second thoughts about the whole project.

"Oh, Laurie," (to my father) "how can we possibly leave them here? Where's the bathroom?"

My father was peering into a glass, opaque with several strata of other people's toothpaste.

"There's a person in the bath," he said. "He seems to be a student chappie. He was asleep. Looked American to me."

Anna said quickly: "It's the season for tourists. Madame did say every available corner was being used."

My father put my suitcase on the bed. The counterpane had once been pink, but that was many layers of grey ago. He said: "Glad we put in some toilet paper. All you'll get here is back numbers of the *Figaro* or the *Herald Tribune*."

"You must both promise," said my mother as they left to creak down five flights of stairs to the ground floor, "to come and bath in our hotel. And keep in touch. And be careful."

"Yes, of course we will," we said. But being careful and bathing was just what we had come to get away from.

Late on Thursday night, August 10th, 1964
Starving is quite fun. It gives you an interest in life. All our mental and physical energies for the last couple of days have been concentrated on food. And money. It's amazing how we take food for granted. We eat, we enjoy it or not as the case

34

may be, and move on to the next thing. That's in normal times. Anna and I have spent a lot of time talking about food.

A sample of our conversation, from late on Wednesday night. (We are in our beds. It's just like being back in the dorm.)

Anna: I wouldn't even say no to school stew.

Me: I could eat it too, I suppose. Yuck! What does Mary always say, horrible creature, as she spears the hideous lumps of gristle on her fork?

Anna and me, in unison: "Is this anyone you know?"

Me: That casserole yesterday was something. Fragrant with herbs, full of actual meat, falling apart in the succulent juices . . .

Anna: Shut up, for heaven's sake!

Silence, punctuated by groans of hunger.

Me: How about that disgusting Spotty Dick? All suety and pale? Dead raisins?

Anna: I could eat it. Even with lumpy custard.

Me: I could eat anything, but I keep thinking of nice things.

Anna: We've done quite well today. Coffee and one baguette to share for breakfast.

Me: Coffee and one helping of chips for lunch.

Anne: Coffee and an apple and some salami for supper. Which was a long time ago.

Me: But we had to buy two books of Metro tickets. And you wanted to send a postcard home. And that's our money for the day used up, if you count paying for the room.

Anna: Tomorrow, we'll do a bit better. No Metro tickets, no postcards. We'll be able to afford some soup. Goodnight.

My night thoughts are very greedy. Paris has to be the foodiest city in the world. You cannot walk two steps here without bumping into a café, being slapped in the face by restaurant smells, or meeting a shop selling something absolutely scrumptious. I could write a book about French cake shops. The fancy cakes look like tiers of well-dressed theatre

35

goers in their best pastel icing, topped with sugared violets and sprays of angelica. There are round, flat tarts, full of concentric circles of apple slices, thin as whispers, or fat little apricot halves, under a sticky glaze of jam. Florentines: bumpy nuts and cherries on top, and silky chocolate underneath. Meringues like puffs of smoke filled with cream. Plastic boxes full of sugared almonds, rum truffles, marrons glacés — I can't go on.

There are other food shops, too. Cheese shops, of course, and meat shops, where you can choose from a hundred different kinds of pâté and sausage. We buy our food in the markets, because they are cheaper. We haggle over the prices and try to avoid looking at the piles of fruit and salad vegetables on every stall.

But we are having fun. There are no bells, and no one tells us what to do. We can sit for hours over one cup of coffee, and watch the people going by, and look at the river, or Nôtre Dame, or the chestnut trees on the boulevards. I feel as if I'm permanently walking about in a painting, everywhere is so lovely. I said as much to Anna yesterday. She thought for a minute and said: "Yes, you do have the look of a Renoir lady, sometimes." That's a nice way of saying Fat is Beautiful. The people, the ones we see sitting about in cafés, or walking in the streets, also bear a striking resemblance to drawings by Toulouse Lautrec or Degas. "Not the tourists," Anna says. She's right, of course. I exclude us from that category.

There are a lot of young Americans about, in plimsolls and T-shirts. They have clean hair and some look a bit like Paul Newman. I'd like to meet some people. Some *boys*, if I'm to be honest, but we haven't yet worked out the right way of going about it. Several men, faintly sinister and grubby, have tried to approach us in the Metro or on the street. My heart pounds, and my throat closes up with fear when this happens, but they have so far beaten a hasty retreat after a selection of Anna's words, not to be found in any A-level vocabulary book that I've ever seen. She drawls them out with a heavy English accent. The effect is devastating. She is also much taller than most of the grubby little men, which may have something to do with it. But we must meet some people.

We have become quite cunning. There are ways of getting things without paying for them. Cigarettes, for instance. Both Anna and I have started to smoke. I don't think either of us likes it very much, but it's part of the image, so we bought a packet of Gauloises in yellow paper on the first day of the Great Famine, and have rationed them strictly, just as if we were in prison. This morning at breakfast we were smoking the last two. Anna's went out while it was resting in the ashtray for a moment. We hunted for matches. No matches. Looking around for a possible light, we noticed an elderly couple smoking at a nearby table. They had about them enough cameras and guide books to assure us that they were tourists, and the lady's sunglasses could only have been, in Anna's words, "products of the New World". She got up, went over to their table with the half-smoked stub, and said in her best BBC voice: "Excuse me, but I wonder whether you could possibly let me have a light? It's dreadfully silly, I know, but I'm afraid I've left my matches behind and this is my very last cigarette." The eyes behind the diamante sunglasses took in a smile, long, dirty hair, and upper class English vowel sounds.

"Why, sure, honey, sure." A match was lit. "And you go ahead and take the rest of these cigarettes, why don't you? We have plenty more back at the hotel, and I guess you kids don't have much money."

"Many, many thanks. You're very kind indeed. Are you enjoying Paris?"

"Why, yes. It sure is full of things to see. But expensive! Wow!" And so it went on for a few more minutes and then Anna returned, bearing a red packet labelled "Marlboro". When our kind benefactors had left, waving to us as they passed, we counted fourteen cigarettes. Treasure!

"They thought we were students," I said, feeling very

37

grown-up.

"Yes." Anna was thoughtful. "We must try that again at lunchtime, that trick."

I'm so thick. Trying it again had never occurred to me. We tried it again. And again. It worked every time. At four o'clock we achieved a packet each from what looked remarkably like a Texan millionaire and his wife.

Sunday morning, August 13th, 1964

Conversation at breakfast.

Anna says: "We must be more systematic. We must know what we want, what kind of person we want to meet, and go straight for them."

I say: "I don't know how you think we'll do that. Dropping hankies is out and we can hardly leer at gentlemen from behind our fans, can we? Anyway, what sort of person do we want? How can you know in advance?"

Anna says: "Of course, I know in advance. You don't believe all that rubbish about eyes meeting across a crowded room, and destiny and stuff, do you?"

I say nothing because, in my deepest heart, I do believe it. Anna goes on: "I want someone British to start with. I don't think romantic adventures should be complicated by language problems."

"American boys always look nice," I venture weakly. Anna sniffs.

She says: "If you like that sort of thing. I think they look like tramps or else like footballers. You know, either appallingly sick or disgustingly healthy."

"I like the way they look in T-shirts."

"Whatever do you mean by that?"

"Oh, I don't know." I know perfectly well, but I'm not explaining if she doesn't know what I'm talking about. I like the way the T-shirt falls from their shoulder blades making patterns of straight, hard lines that change when they walk. And I like their white teeth.

"Anyway," Anna goes on, "let's put it like this — you

wouldn't say 'no' to a Britisher?''

"No, I suppose not, but I had hoped for something a little more exotic. I could meet English boys at home."

"We haven't exactly been sweeping swooning suitors off the doorstep, though, have we? Nigel of the clammy hands and Peter of the bow legs and disappearing chin? All that lot?''

"O.K. I give in. Tell me your plan, though I don't see why the people we meet here are guaranteed against vanishing chins, hairlines, etc.''

"Right," says Anna. "Look at this." (She takes out a little flag.) "It got me tons of lifts on the way here. The Union Jack will be our passport to romance. We'll put it on the table when we eat.''

"What's eating?''

"Shush. Let me finish. We'll put it up, and all English men for miles around will flock to the ancient flag. You'll see. They won't be able to help it.''

"Americans will flock too. They may, anyway. They'll know we can speak English, at least.''

"Which is more than many of them can.''

"Oh, don't be so silly, Anna. You're not even funny sometimes with your put-on snobbishness.''

"Tut, tut. What you need is a square meal.''

"You can say that again.''

"I can, but I shan't. Let's go and decide where not to go for lunch.''

We leave the table. I'm going to telephone my parents and arrange for baths. If all these gorgeous chaps are going to rally to the standard when we stick it in the salt pot, then I, for one, am going to be as fragrant and petal-soft as a lady in a soap commercial.

Sunday night, August 13th, 1964

Well, we put the flag up at dinner, and what we got was Jim Charlton, a nineteen-year-old student from Liverpool. Brown hair, *à la Beatles*, blue anorak, tatty blue jeans and guitar.

Ordinary looking. He plays the guitar. It is not just for show. He is quite nice, really. We all had an extra cup of coffee to celebrate meeting in a foreign land. I'm glad my hair was clean. I'm glad the café had a dim light, kind to spotty faces. I'm glad I was wearing my mother's red blouse. Jim is a student of mathematics. He must be very clever. But let me tell it all in the right order. First, the baths. We fixed it so that we arrived at lunchtime and joined my parents in a restaurant near their hotel. After we had finished eating, my mother said: "Jill, that's the first meal you've eaten in total silence since you were three months old. You must be very hungry."

"Not any more, thank you. Though I could probably squash in a crème caramel."

"How about you, Anna dear?"

"I could manage one, I think. Just. Thank you very much."

I wrapped some pieces of bread in a napkin, and put them into my bag while my parents were paying the bill.

Then came the baths. Oh, Glory be! We each took hours wallowing, stroking the clean enamel, splashing under the shining silver taps, conjuring up mountains of lather from the pink soap, drifting in avalanches of talcum powder. We used up about six towels, and took ages, each of us, to scrub the bath afterwards. An astonishing amount of dirt was shed that day. Then we took turns at the dressing table, plastering our faces with lotions, creams, lipstick and eye shadow, and helping ourselves to my mother's "Arpège". At the end, I may not have looked much like her, but I felt like Brigitte Bardot.

Later, in the café, we put the flag into the salt cellar and waited. Jim came almost immediately.

"Hello," he said. "You English? I haven't spoken to anyone in English for days, and that's a fact. Can I sit down, and so on?"

"Yes," we said, "please do."

We talked for hours. Then we went back to our room, and

40

Jim played the guitar, and I sang. Lovely songs. Joan Baez and Bob Dylan songs. A few by the Beatles. Simon and Garfunkel, that kind of thing. Then we stopped to have a cigarette. Jim looked at me and said: ''That's a hell of a voice you've got there. We could all be rolling, thanks to you.''

''Thank you,'' I said. ''What do you mean rolling?''

''Busking is what I mean. You know, you sing outside the cafés and I play and Anna goes round with the hat.''

''I daren't.''

''Why not? Give pleasure to a lot of people. Of course, we'll have to watch out for *les flics*.''

''Cops? Why? Is it illegal?'' I was certainly not up to breaking the law.

''Well, you know, frowned on. They move you on, that's all. Just have to go somewhere else.''

''You sound as if you'd done it before,'' said Anna.

''Not so good, me on my own. It's Jill's voice. That's what'll make the money. It's one hell of a voice.''

The blushes were breaking like waves over my face by now. But the plan was made. Rehearsals tomorrow, opening night Tuesday, and Wednesday, the world would be our oyster, according to Jim.

Sunday night, August 20th, 1964
It is all, as they say, happening. A proper rags to riches saga. I didn't believe it at first. But it seems that people will actually pay money (money that you can buy cakes with, imagine!) to hear me sing. I was nervous at first. I sang quite loudly to rise above the noise of cars, and fixed my eyes on Anna, walking among the tables with her straw hat ready for coins. And then the tables faded away, and the music shook me, and I forgot where I was in the joy of raising my voice above the talk and the traffic and the whole street and high over the awning into the sky, with nothing but strummed chords on the guitar for company. When I had finished, and when we had counted the money in the hat (which we did round the corner, discreetly), I realized that four songs had earned us enough to pay for a

proper meal, each, in a cheap restaurant. It seemed impossible. Jim jumped up and down and kissed me noisily on the cheek, shouting: "A goldmine, that's what she is — a proper bloody goldmine!" We did go and eat, but I was so excited, I couldn't finish the food. It was the kiss that did for me, I think, not being called a goldmine. Nothing very romantic about that. Anna said at one point: "Jill's not eating. That's never happened before. She must be in love." Then she giggled. I would have murdered her if the knife had been sharper.

From that night on, we were more and more successful. We worked out a route of cafés, all the way down the Boulevard St. Michel to the river, velvet in the dark, and then up the Rue Saint Jacques to our home ground near the Pantheon. Mostly we collected coins, but there were an awful lot of them. We ate heartily every night, we could afford croissants at breakfast, and we stopped scrounging for cigarettes. Also, we made friends. Young Americans followed us and came to sit at our table after we had finished singing for the night. It grew to be a sort of gang, and we always called them The Gang when we talked about them privately, Anna and I. I felt so sophisticated and intellectual talking about Rimbaud and Baudelaire at two in the morning, to handsome young men with scholarships to the Sorbonne. I thanked my lucky stars for *Twelve French Poets*, the A-level syllabus, and our rectangular French teacher, who was so thorough that I found I could discuss symbolism and synaesthesia without batting an eyelid. I began to understand Rimbaud very well: Rimbaud, who at my age had invented the colours of vowels. He understood what it meant to be sixteen. He knew about light-hearted people walking under lime trees on pale, summer evenings and falling in love for a while, not very seriously. He knew about wanting huge and overwhelming experiences. And he wrote a sonnet about a plate of ham and a mug of beer he had once tasted, after walking for miles and miles. You can almost reach into the poem and pick the food up from the plate.

42

One night, a crowd gathered behind me on the pavement. Anna went round with the hat to these people also. Then suddenly an old man pushed his way through to me and shook my hand. An American. He said: "May the Good Lord take a likin' to ya!" and disappeared into the crowd. He stopped near Anna, though, for a moment and dropped a ten franc note into the hat. Nearly a pound. We fingered it with awe. It was our first paper money. That night, we bought coffees for The Gang.

Monday night, August 21st, 1964

Today we went to lunch with my parents. Jim came too, for the second time. My parents were quite bewildered to hear of our success. I said that we would make the trip to Montparnasse one night and sing around the "Coupole" and the "Dome" for Reggie, my parents and their friends, but my father said he would pay us a lot of money to stay away. He said he would have died of embarrassment. Jim assured him that hearing me sing was the experience of a lifetime, but Dad wasn't having that. Busking was undignified, he said, and if I wanted to do it, then fine, but not anywhere near him, thank you very much. Tonight is my night off. Anna has gone to the movies with Mark, one of The Gang. Tomorrow, I shall make her eat, on toast and with ketchup, every word she has ever said about the men of the New World. Jim has gone to meet a friend of his who is supposed to be coming from Liverpool. I could have gone down to the café and talked literature with the lads, but there didn't seem to be much point without Jim and Anna. What I really mean is, without Jim. Am I in love? I think I might be. I get a lot of butterflies in my stomach. I'm thinner. Tears come to my eyes when I sing songs about saying goodbye, or faithless lovers, or anything like that. After singing "Don't think twice, it's all right", Dylan's greatest song, my heart feels like shredded cabbage. I think I must be in love. I don't think Jim is, though. Ordinary, funny, practical and friendly, but far from loving. Apart from that kiss the first night we busked together, there has been nothing.

I've gone over and over that kiss in my mind and come to the conclusion that it was the kind of exhuberant gesture that footballers bestow on goal-scorers. Elated. Not lover-like at all. I wish I knew how to flirt. It comes naturally to some people, but there should be night-school classes in it for the rest of us. There's not long left. Next Saturday night will be my last night in Paris. Soon, Anna and I will be back at school. Rimbaud will look quite different, pressed into the hard, blue covers of a book.

The tail-end of a conversation in the early hours of Tuesday morning.

Anna says: "But will you still be my friend? I mean, I like you, and we get on and everything. Will this make any difference?"

I say: "I suppose not. Not in the long run. I mean, you couldn't help yourselves. That's what you keep saying. And anyway, I never said. And Jim never said. I wish you'd told me sooner, that's all. And you didn't both have to lie to me about tonight. Give yourselves alibis."

Anna says: "Mark likes you, I know he does."

I say: "*Everybody* likes me! Everybody LIKES me! I'm fed up to here with being liked and admired and called a proper bloody goldmine and the next Barbra Streisand. I want to look like a racehorse and have long hair and Jim, that's what I want. What use is being liked, for heaven's sake?"

Silence from Anna. I say: "Sorry, Anna. I know it's not your fault. And of course we'll be friends. That'd be terrific, wouldn't it, losing Jim and you in one swell foop, as they say. Terrific."

Anna says: "Will you go on singing, though? Will you be able to?"

I say: "Sing? Of course I shall sing. I'm a trouper, aren't I? On with the motley, the show must go on, smile though your heart is breaking and other assorted clichés."

44

Anna says: "You're a nice person, Jill."
I say: "And a fat lot of good it does me."

Friday night, August 25th, 1964

There it is, it's finished. Tonight was positively the last appearance on the pavements of Paris of Jill Simpson, the outsize wondergirl. I thought I managed very well considering that tears were running down my cheeks most of the time. The last few days have been dreadful. Jim *will* walk with his arm round Anna's waist, and they tend to vanish if you turn away for a moment. Later on, they reappear. The look on their faces is like that on the faces of parents at Christmas time, when they know what the presents are and you don't.

My suitcase is packed. Tomorrow I will go on the boat train with my parents. Anna and Jim are staying on. I shall see Anna at school. My father told me a joke once, about a man who marries an ugly opera singer because he loves her voice. On the first morning of their honeymoon, he wakes up early and looks at the lady, still sleeping on the pillow beside him. He wakes her gently, and as she opens her eyes, he says to her: "Sing, darling, sing!" I think that's what might happen to me.

4. Bounce the Moon

Shorehaven in November was deserted. Striped deck-chairs had gone from the long, grey stretch of shingle below the Promenade, and the fairy-lights that spiralled around the white lampposts were never turned on after the beginning of October for reasons of economy. The Pier, its roof frivolously decorated with wrought-iron curlicues, stood silently in slate-grey water, now that the summer clicking and whirring of the many slot machines had stopped. Away from the front, the Park was messy with autumn: dead leaves, soggy from the rain, littered the smooth grass and lay around the renowned Rose Garden ("whose glorious show of colour is always much enjoyed by visitors"). Apart from one or two struggling and shrivelled survivors, the roses were no more than a memory.

Near the Park, just on the edge of a tangled network of streets full of bed-and-breakfast houses, stood the Tivoli Theatre. The creamy paint on its plaster columns was peeling. The once-scarlet, once-thick carpet in the foyer had been trodden down to a greasy thinness the exact shade of hard, encrusted blood. Nevertheless, the Tivoli was alive. Bright blue posters announced the opening of a pantomime. An old favourite "Cinderella". People came in and out of the glass doors. Bright stockings, and long hair, and trousers in untrouserlike colours like pink and lemon yellow, velvet jackets, loud voices and laughter, warned the staider citizens of Shorehaven that actors had arrived in their midst, an exotic flock of migrant birds whose fine plumage mocked the grey and tan and black that they had adopted as camouflage for the winter months.

Grace Stockwell was not one of the staider citizens. She sat in the front room of her house (Arcadia Villas, Bed and Breakfast) pouring tea for the wickedly handsome young man on the sofa, who had taken a room for the entire run of the pantomime. As soon as she'd seen him, Grace had known he was an actor. Only an actor's hair could fall across his brow with just that air of studied abandon, only an actor could ask her if she had a room available in just those tones of highwayman, doomed poet and pathetic little boy all rolled into one.

She crossed her remarkably elegant legs, silky in high-heeled patent-leather shoes, and smiled in fair imitation of a Hollywood siren as she handed the cup across the table to Miles. That was the young man's name, and within minutes of crossing the threshold, he had insisted on being one of the family.

"I used to be on the stage myself," said Grace, "a long time ago. Before Miranda was born. Of course, after my husband died, I had to find work that would enable me to look after her, and this did seem ideal."

"I could tell," Miles said. "You can always tell a stage person. You have the style. The vivacity."

Grace laughed. "I have tried to avoid being the kind of theatrical landlady one reads about. You know, old posters on the wall, signed photographs and so on. Too boring, really. A cliché."

"Absolutely," Miles agreed. "You're not a bit like anyone's idea of a landlady. How old is your little girl?"

"She's sixteen," said Grace.

"I don't believe it," said Miles. "You can't possibly . . . I mean, I'm sorry . . ." he looked at Grace out of blue eyes fringed with ridiculously long lashes. "It's just that you don't look much more than seventeen yourself."

"Flatterer!"

"No, it's true. Really."

"Well, I did have Miranda when I was very young."

"If she's anything like you, she must be a knockout."

"You," said Grace, mock-severely (her heart was flutter-
ing quite uncomfortably and she could feel a most immature
desire to blush and simper rising within her), "are a naughty
boy, and I shall have to keep you in your place, I can see
that." She shook a finger at him. "There's Miranda now,
back from school." She jumped up from her chair. "I'll just
go and tell her we're here."

Miranda lay in bed and thought about Miles. Perhaps he
was lying in his bed upstairs and thinking about her. She
smiled into the darkness. The minute he saw her, he'd fallen
to his knees and kissed her hand. No one had ever done that
before. He had called her a princess, and vowed that she was
every bit as beautiful as her mother, and he wouldn't know
(such would be his terrible dilemma) where to bestow his
heart. Well, it had all been acting, of course. He didn't mean
it. But later he had talked to her and she had told him how
she, too, wanted, indeed was determined to be an actress one
day, and he had looked quite serious, and offered to take her to
watch a rehearsal and meet the cast. He sounded as though he
meant it. He sounded concerned, anxious to please her.
Miranda had wished she was that little bit taller, slimmer,
more elegant, wished she had washed her hair that morning,
wished wished wished with all her heart that the completely
miraculous would happen and Miles would fall in love with
her. She, of course, had plunged, dived, tumbled, plummeted
heart-first straight into desperate love for Miles as soon as she
had seen him. And why not? Wasn't he gorgeous? Wasn't
he totally different from the boys who had fumblingly and
rather horridly and wetly, she thought, kissed her and said
they quite fancied her? Wasn't he an actor? A person whose
whole life was devoted to his art? Love with such a person,
Miranda knew, would be exactly as she had imagined it:
ringed with radiance, and tenderness and glamour, larger
than life, more brightly-coloured, just like the movies. She
could see it all. Falling asleep, she had a clear picture (close-
up) of her mouth and Miles' perfect mouth drawing closer

and closer together, to the accompaniment of swelling, soaring, unseen music.

Grace was taking off her make-up, singing softly to herself:
  "The moment that you speak
  I want to go play hide and seek,
  I want to go and bounce the moon
  Just like a toy balloon . . ."
She peered into the mirror. Not bad. That silly young man with his nonsense. "You look like sisters," he had said, when Miranda came in. She, poor kid, was smitten. That was obvious. Grace hoped that it would not all end in tears. Miles was a heartbreaker, and no mistake. Why, she thought, if I were younger, I'd be smitten myself. Such lovely hands. Long fingers, and a sensitive person too. Look how he had talked to Miranda, and offered to take her to rehearsal. How kind that was of him. Grace took off her peignoir (fringed with feathers: a little touch of luxury. Everyone needed such things from time to time,) and slid into bed. Thoughts of Miles and Miranda together at rehearsal came into her mind, and that made her feel, she could not quite analyse how they made her feel. Perhaps uncomfortable was the word. What nonsense! Miranda is still a child, she thought. Miles must be twenty-five if he's a day. He wouldn't look at her. She's just a kid to him. But the uncomfortable feeling remained, and to cheer herself up, Grace began to plan what she would wear tomorrow. Was the pink too short? Perhaps a little too clinging round the hips? But pink suits me, she thought, and what the hell, my hips are still trim enough to be clung to. The clingier the better.

The sun had risen above a bank of puffy blue clouds that lay along the horizon. It was only a pallid disc in the sky, shedding thin white light through the still air on to the faces of a few well-wrapped-up and elderly people, who sat on the benches along the Promenade, taking the air. The letters on the front of the Tivoli theatre should have been picked out in light bulbs, but the "L" and the "O" were broken. This morning, two workmen were half-heartedly screwing new bulbs into the sockets. The dark clouds had crept up from the sea, and trailed across the sky. Soon, they would catch up with the sun and obscure it. Perhaps it would rain later.

Miranda hardly ever got up for breakfast at the weekends, but on Miles' first morning she appeared punctually at half past eight.

"'It is the East, and Juliet is the sun,'" Miles declaimed, waving toast and marmalade in the air.

"Wrong play," said Miranda. "It's *The Tempest* you want."

"Your beauty," (Miles bit into the toast and crunched it up, managing to smile at the same time), "coming so early in the morning, and so on, is totally confusing. After all," he added, smiling at Grace as she brought in another pot of tea, "my poor bewildered senses have already suffered one assault at the hands of your delicious mother."

Miranda blushed. Her mother was wearing the pink jersey thing that stuck to her all over. And a touch of perfume. And, oh God, she was going into her Lauren Bacall routine. She leaned against the door, shook her hair over her face, and lowered her eyelids.

"If you want anything," she growled throatily, "just whistle. You know how to whistle, don't you?"

Miles roared with laughter, and clapped his hands. "Bloody marvellous, really. Grace, you're terrific."

Her mother curtsied. Miranda wished devoutly that she would stop showing off, that she would behave . . . well, like other mothers. That she would be a little less like a young woman. She wasn't young. She was thirty-nine. That was old. Mothers were not supposed to flirt. That's what she's doing, thought Miranda, suddenly furious. She's flirting with Miles. How could she? However could she? She looked ridiculous. Stupid. Miles didn't seem to mind, that was the worst of it. Miles seemed to like it. Miranda cut her toast with such force that a corner of it flew on to the floor. She wished her mother would leave the room, leave her alone with Miles. She sat quite quietly, listening to their banter, transfixed by Miles' hair and the way it fell on to his neck, mesmerized by trying to imagine the smooth body under the blue polo-necked sweater.

The interior of the Tivoli Theatre was a far cry from Drury Lane, but Miranda didn't mind. What did it matter if the gilded cherubs on the ceiling were chipped and almost brown, or if the seats all looked stricken with a terrible disease that left huge, bald patches where the plush should have been? As soon as the lights, amber and pink and blue, were turned on, the dusty stage became a magic place. She sat in the stalls and watched the director, a thin, bald man with a gingery beard whose name was Vic or Mick or Dick or something, take the company through Act One of the show. Miles didn't seem to have very much to do in the bits she watched. She had brief glimpses of him in the wings, his head unpleasantly close to the head of a girl called Mona who was playing Prince Charming. Mona was tall, and bosomy and dark, with flashing teeth and a very red mouth. I'm colourless next to her, thought Miranda. If I didn't have long hair, everyone would think I was a boy. After the rehearsal they all, Miranda too, went to the Adelphi tea-rooms, where they laughed at the décor: "Straight from the thirties, darling. Can you believe it?" "This whole town has been in aspic since before the war. Jellied. Perfectly preserved," and spoke in loud, happy voices. Nobody talked to her in particular, but she was sitting opposite Miles and, from time to time, a smile flew roughly in her direction, for which she was grateful.

Later, Miranda and Miles walked back to Arcadia Villas together along the Promenade. It was a windy evening, with rain in the air. The sea grumbled and crashed over the stony beach, and blew salt in their faces. The moon was hidden by clouds and the street-lights reflected yellow on the pavement, damp from the spray and earlier showers.

"What did you think of them all, then?" asked Miles.

"Lovely," said Miranda; "I did enjoy it. Thanks for taking me. I think you should have more to do, though."

Miles laughed: "Oh, wait till you see Act Two. I have a whole song then. I'm pining away for Cinders, you see. Listen." They stopped walking and Miranda gazed at Miles as he broke into full song. Here on the Promenade, she thought. Anyone could hear. How does he dare? She listened to the words:

"If I can dance an endless dance with you,
And take the road to true romance with you,
Our lips entwined
Our hearts as one,
Then I will love you when the dance was done."

Miranda clapped when the song was over, came down to earth. For a moment, when Miles had looked so meltingly at her as those words poured from him, it seemed as though he were speaking to her, and the dark, wet night simply faded away from around her, and she was transported to a warm summer garden on the night of a Royal Ball.

"Dreadful words, really," Miles said, as they walked on.

"I thought you were . . ." Miranda hesitated. What could she say? ". . . very good."

"You are a loyal and lovely person," said Miles seriously, and turned to face her. Quite suddenly, out of the blue, really, he brought his mouth very close to hers, and kissed her, gently and tenderly. Miranda thought she would faint. Forever, she thought. I shall remember this first kiss forever. Here, by this bench, under this particular special lamppost, Miles kissed me. I shall think of it every time I pass it. This is our lamppost, our bench. Heavenly bliss, rapture and glory. Miranda walked on next to Miles. He was chatting away happily, about his plans for next season, next year, the year after, and Miranda hardly heard him.

The sea was angry. Dark blue and flecked with white. Curling and twisting. Sucking at loose shingle, and tossing spray high into the air. All day, the wind blew, sighing and lamenting through the town, until about three o'clock, when it retired exhausted. The sky had been swept clean. In the twilight it seemed to shine a pale, opalescent blue, nearly white.

The Box Office lady at the Tivoli theatre adjusted the hair she had so carefully twisted into two buns over her ears, pushed her glasses up her nose, and opened her cash-box, ready for the first night crowds.

"Grace, darling," said Miles, "you honestly shouldn't. Not cuff links like these. They're too much."

"Just a little present to celebrate your first night. We both thought you were marvellous. And so kind to let us come to the party afterwards. Miranda was in heaven. And aren't all your friends lovely?"

"Not as lovely as you, Grace."

"Now, now," Grace blushed. "Let's just put on those cuff links and see how they look."

"You do too much for me," said Miles, as Grace fiddled with his shirt-sleeves. "All those books, and that super record, and that lovely silk shirt . . . it's really naughty of you."

"Well," said Grace, "we've grown very attached to you, Miranda and I." She turned his hands over, still holding them in her own. "There, don't they look lovely."

"It's you who are lovely, Grace." Miles knelt at her side, and slid his arms around her, kissing her neck, "Please Grace."

She struggled half-heartedly. "No, Miles, I can't. Miranda will be coming in in a minute. I can't. Oh, Miles, please . . . I shouldn't . . .'' Miles turned her face to him, and kissed her hard and decisively.

"You can, Grace. You must. I can't bear it. You're so lovely."

"Not now," Grace sighed, "later, maybe."

"Promise?" Miles took her in his arms again, ran his tongue over her lips.

"I promise," Grace whispered. "Yes, I promise."

On Sunday, Miranda and her friend Carol had spent the morning setting each other's hair. It was nearly lunch-time when Miranda came home. She could hear her mother singing in the kitchen:

"You and I
Are just like a couple of tots.
Running across the meadow
Picking up lots of forget-me-nots."

"Hello," she said, opening the door to the kitchen. "Oh. Why are you still in your dressing-gown? Are you ill?"

"No, my child, I am not ill. I am hunky-dory and peachy-creamy and this, I would have you know, is a peignoir and not a slummocky old dressing-gown."

"What about lunch?"

"Ah me, the young! You think of nothing but your stomachs." Grace grinned. "We will live dangerously for once. We will send out for fish and chips. Down with roast beef and two veg! Down with Sunday Dinner!"

"But what have you been doing? You were up when I left. You gave me breakfast. You must have been doing something."

This struck Grace as immensely funny. For a few moments she was laughing so much she couldn't speak. In the end, wiping the tears from her eyes, she giggled weakly: "I went back to bed. That's what I did. I went back to bed."

Miranda, despairing of ever understanding her mother, sighed.

"Oh, well. I guess I'll have to get the fish and chips. I'm starving." The sound of her mother singing followed her down the hall:

"You make me feel there are songs to be sung
Bells to be rung
And a wonderful fling to be flung . . ."

The rain began on Monday morning and showed no signs of ever stopping. There was nothing interesting or spectacular about it. It was simply grey water in a steady stream falling on to a sea the colour of metal, on to a grey town.

Outside the Tivoli Theatre, it was raining on the photographs (behind glass) of all the pantomime stars. Rivers of raindrops created the illusion that all the faces were melting, were weeping.

The pantomime was in its second week. Saturday was the last night, and Miles would be leaving on Monday. Miranda sat in her room feeling thoroughly miserable, and going back over and over again in her head every single significant thing that Miles had said or done since that first time he kissed her on the Promenade. It wasn't much. After the first night, at the party he had danced with her three times, and ruffled her hair once. A few days ago, they had had a long and intense discussion about acting, and he had read through some scenes with her, and told her she had great talent and great beauty. After the matinée, she had met him for tea, and he had held her hand, and looked soulful, and told her how innocent she was and how easy it would be to fall in love with her, but how he mustn't, he couldn't, because he would be leaving and it wouldn't be fair to her, and anyway, he had his career to think of, etc. It could be interpreted either way. A declaration of love, or the cold shoulder. Perhaps I ought, she thought, to offer to run away with him, forget about A-levels and auditions for RADA and my own career. But I can't. I want to act so much. Does that mean I don't love him? She considered this. Maybe I don't love him enough? But how could I possibly love anyone more? Last night, Miles had kissed her in the pantry. Properly. Thinking about it even now made her

55

tremble. She had spent the whole day, today, hoping it might happen again, but it hadn't. Perhaps it was a kind of farewell kiss. Maybe, she thought, I should go up there and offer myself to him. The thought made her blush, and anyway, how awful if he refused her. Miranda kicked her dressing-table, feeling murderous. If only some miracle could happen. If only the pantomime could go on for ever. If only Grace were in a mood slightly more in tune with her own. What made everything worse, Miranda decided, was that while she grew more and more despondent, Grace seemed to be getting happier and happier. It wasn't fair.

The crowd had thinned out now and only a few people were left, dancing in a desultory fashion on the dimly-lit stage. Make-up had run and faded, shoulder straps were drooping, the music was slow and sleepy, so that the dancers seemed to be twined together in a kind of trance. Miranda yawned. She had drunk some punch. Not too much. Grace had seen to that, but it was late and as she sat on the King's throne in the wings, she wished with all her heart that she could be in bed. It had been a horrible party. Miles had been surrounded all evening, it seemed, by droves of tinselled ladies. He had only danced with her once, a fast number that involved a lot of flashy twirling and spinning and no holding at all. I must find Grace, she thought. Or Miles. Someone to come home with me. She peered on to the stage, but they weren't there. Wearily, she began to look for them all over the theatre. She found them in the Green Room. They were on the sofa, all curled up together, kissing, really kissing and her mother was making strange noises. Her mother and Miles. Miranda fled, unseeing down the dark passage to the lavatory where she sat for a very long time feeling sick to her stomach. Several times she thought she would vomit, but nothing came. Later, she wandered back to the stage. Her mother was talking to the director as though nothing had happened. Perhaps I imagined it, she thought.

''Come on lovey,'' said her mother in an absolutely

normal voice, "beddy-byes for both of us. I feel worn out, and I'll tell you something."

"What?"

"I've had a few too many."

Miranda felt an immense relief come over her. A few too many, that was all it was. People never knew what they were doing properly when they were drunk. That was all right then.

Snow had fallen, frosting the rooftops, lying along the tops of hedges and muffling the faraway sound of the icy sea.

In a side street behind the Tivoli Theatre, men in woollen hats and overalls carried flats painted with chandeliers, terraces, staircases, Cinderella's kitchen, and pushed them nonchalantly into the dark interior of a parked truck. Wicker skips full of silks and satins, wigs and ruffled skirts and Cinderella's rags, were bundled inside, and the truck drove away. The snow began to fall again.

"I wonder what's happened to Miles," Grace yawned. "He's probably as hung over as I am, but still, if he doesn't get here soon, there'll be no breakfast."

"Shall I go up and see?" Miranda asked.

"Yes, that's a good idea. Here, take him up a cup of tea."

Miranda left the room quickly, so that her mother should not see the redness that covered her face and neck at the very thought of seeing Miles in bed . . . in pyjamas. Maybe he didn't even wear pyjamas. Miranda nearly let go of the cup she was carrying. She knocked on Miles' door. There was no answer. She knocked again. Nothing. He must have been very, very tired last night. Slowly, she opened the door as quietly as she could.

"Mum," she shouted. "Mum, come up here! He's gone. He's not here. Oh, Mum, come *on*!"

A pale-faced Grace ran up the stairs. "What do you mean,

gone? Where, for Heaven's sake? How?'' She stood in the doorway. The sheets and blankets were neatly folded on the mattress, the drawers were open, and the cupboard door hung ajar. There were no clothes inside. There was not one single trace of Miles in the room. It was as though he had never been.

Miranda began to cry. Her mother turned on her.

''And what the hell do you think you're crying about? Hey? I'm the one who should be crying. I'm the one he's robbed. Yes, robbed. The swine owes me for two weeks. I said he could pay later. I'm a bloody fool. Oh, Miranda, for God's sake, stop that snivelling. I can't bear it. I'm the one . . .'' Suddenly, Grace crumpled on to the bed in a torrent of tears so violent and overwhelming that Miranda stopped crying at once. She had never seen her mother cry. Not properly. No more than damp eyes quickly wiped during a sad film.

''Mum, don't cry. It doesn't matter about the money. It doesn't really matter about Miles. We'll soon forget . . .'' For a moment, Miranda saw herself as one of those lovely heroines who could never forget, who pined away beautifully on velvet chaise-longues. Her mother sat up suddenly and started shouting through the tears.

''What do you know about it? You'll just never know. He robbed me. Not the money. I'm not talking about the bloody money. He's taken the very last shreds of my youth. He made me feel young . . . beautiful . . . and it was all nothing, just nothing, just acting. Nothing. He didn't mean it. None of it. I thought he was different. I thought he really loved me. Well, I've been a bloody fool and no mistake. A bloody stupid fool.''

Miranda could hardly speak.

''You mean . . . he said that . . . he loved you?''

''Said?'' Her mother laughed. ''He did more than say it, I can tell you. Much more.''

All at once, Miranda remembered her mother still in a dressing-gown at lunchtime that Sunday. What had she said? She said she'd been back to bed. But with Miles? Surely, oh surely not with Miles. She had to ask. Directly. She could scarcely bring the words into her mouth. They revolted her.

"Were you . . . you know . . . lovers?"

Her mother wiped her eyes. "I never meant for you to find out . . ."

"Well, it's a bit bloody late, isn't it?" shrieked Miranda. "A bit bloody late. I think it's disgusting, that's what I think. I can't bear it. It's vile. How can I ever . . . oh, I don't know how you could, it's horrible. Horrible, horrible."

"Horrible, is it? Is that what you think? How dare you? Think you've bloody cornered the market in love, don't you? All you young people. There was nothing horrible about it at all. It was marvellous. Fantastic. What are you gawping at, anyway? I'm thirty-nine, dammit. I'm young, young, young! There's nothing to stop me loving someone. Nothing. And you. What right have you got to judge me? I'll tell you something else. I know how you feel. I've been there and I know, and my heart is sore all over for you, but just catch you feeling the smallest jot of sympathy for me. Oh, no, that would never do, would it? Love's O.K. when it's you in the starring rôle, but me — that's vile and disgusting. Right, if that's what you think, you don't have to stay here. Go to your room. Go out, I don't care. Just go."

"I'll go and make some tea for us," said Miranda in a small voice.

The tea was cold by the time that Grace came down. She had washed her face and put on new make-up.

"Miranda . . ."

"Mum . . ." they both spoke together.

"You first," said Miranda.

"Very well. Here goes," said Grace and took a deep breath. "I'm sorry I yelled at you like a fish wife. I was upset. I'm better now. I'll try and behave in a more grown-up fashion . . ."

"No, it's my fault," said Miranda. "I was jealous. I loved him. I couldn't bear the thought that it was you he loved. But I know how you must feel. I can imagine it. I'm sorry I said all those things. You're not old. I know that, really, but it's because you're my mother. I feel funny about it. I never thought of you as a proper person before. You know, like other people.''

"I know. I know. I really never meant you to find out. I should have been more careful what I said . . . but finding Miles gone like that. I'll tell you what I think.''

"What?''

"We're both better off without a cad like that. In the long run.''

"But it's the short run, that's what hurts, doesn't it?''

"Like hell, love. Like all hell. But the show, as they say, must go on. Smile though your heart is breaking, etc.''

"Yes,'' said Miranda, trying to comfort herself by thinking of other young men. At RADA, there would be many lovely actors. She would be a good actress. She would stand on a pink-lit stage and blow kisses to the gallery. She would succeed. It would be all right.

Grace went into the kitchen to make more tea. Later, she thought. Later, I'll wash those sheets and clean up the room. To hell with Miles anyway. Who needed him? Suddenly, Grace felt very old. Old and wise.

By Sunday evening, all the snow had turned to slush. The waitresses in the Adelphi Tearooms wished that the pantomime were still on. Those young people, well, they did talk a bit loudly and show off, but they always had a smile and a pleasant word, and they did brighten the place up a bit, you couldn't deny it. Still, there'd be another panto next year, and once this spell of bad weather was over, well, it'd nearly be springtime, wouldn't it?

5. Monday

On this particular Monday morning, Adrian had the feeling that he had woken up in a colour supplement. Everything about the kitchen — things he normally did not notice — annoyed him. All the pine fittings, the Habitat china, the split-level cooker (catch his mother leaving the slightest speck of human-looking grease on it!) the vast expanse of lawn stretching away there outside the window for yard after smooth yard: it all made him feel sick. His father, smelling of Old Spice and wearing a pin-striped suit, had left for work in the maroon Jaguar, and his mother was upstairs in her bathroom, plastering over the cracks in her face with stuff out of a bottle. I haven't got time before school, Adrian thought. Pity. I'd like to make a fry-up of eggs, bacon, sausage and beans, and leave splattered fat all over the place and traces of ketchup on my plate. That'd teach her. Maybe one day I will, but not today. He took a yoghurt from the fridge. It was like a supermarket in there — every stupid flavour under the sun. Adrian had taken the first one he came to, which turned out to be Black Cherry. That was O.K. Perhaps it was a good omen. He ate it standing up by the sink, and deliberately left the little pot on the marble work surface. His mother would come down after he'd gone and go ''Tsk, tsk'', and smile indulgently at his messy habits. She wouldn't understand that it was supposed to be a protest. His stomach lurched at the thought of today. It was like exams, only worse. For a moment he thought of being ill, but he couldn't be ill for ever. He'd have to face Helen sooner or later, so better sooner. Helen. How was he going to put it? What would she do? I've never done this kind of thing before, he thought. I don't know the rules. I don't know how it's done. But I must do it. Today. Every day I leave it, it'll get worse. Think of Carol.

"I'm off, Mum," he shouted up the stairs.

"Are you, darling?" his mother trilled back. (Such silver tones could never properly shout.) "Have a lovely day."

"Fat chance," Adrian muttered as he left the house, and aimed a hefty kick at the poor, defenceless geraniums growing tastefully beside the front door in a barrel painted carefully all over in Dulux Brilliant White.

"Have we run out of muesli, Mum?" Helen wrinkled her nose.

"'Fraid so," her mother answered, "Corn Flakes in plenty, though, and you could do yourself an egg if you've got time." She took a sip of coffee.

"You're filling yourself with poisons," said Helen. "Look at you. Coffee, cigarettes, I don't know what else, but probably loaded with cholesterol."

Helen's mother giggled. "Spot on, love. Cream cheese on toast. With butter. Hardens the arteries something chronic. Trouble with your generation is you all know too much for your own good. In my day . . ."

Helen laughed. "I know: steak four times a day topped with butter and tons of eggs and cheese and stuff and you're none the worse for it."

"Right. Listen, Helen, I've got to fly. I've got a nine-thirty tutorial and I'm dropping Kathy off at school first. Don't bother with the dishes. They'll wait till I get home. I'll be back about five-thirty, I expect. Kathy's going to the Bradshaws, so you don't have to worry about her. Thank goodness your father's coming back on Saturday. I find all these arrangements about fetching and carrying absolutely mind-destroying."

Helen followed her mother into the hall. Kathy came downstairs with her long hair in what Helen called "the Gretchen style": two plaits pinned neatly on top of her head.

"I might be back late tonight," Helen said.

"Right," said her mother "but don't miss supper without 'phoning. Adrian, is it?"

Helen smiled. "Yes, it is."

"O.K. We're off then, love. Have a good day."

The house was very quiet after they had gone. It was still early. Helen stood at the window, drinking apple juice and thinking about Adrian. Beautiful Adrian. Too good looking, too blond to be called "handsome". You had to say beautiful. It was the only word which felt right. Clever Adrian, teacher's pet for every teacher. Rich Adrian, who looked as if he ought to be at public school, only his parents didn't believe in it, even though they had pots of cash. Adrian, Adrian, nobody else's Adrian. Just hers.

Mike had got the breakfast routine down to a fine art. Get up with Mum, have a coffee with her before she went off to the early shift, lay the table, shout up to the little ones to get up or else, put the bacon on the grill, put the beans in the pan, butter the bread, boil the kettle. Then, make sure Stevie ate his bread, watch Gary to see he didn't pinch the beans off Jenny's plate, talk to Patrick to see he didn't fall asleep again and keep an eye out for fights, punches, kicks under the table and flying crusts. Then get the whole lot into their coats ready to march off to school, which was only round the corner. Then back to the kitchen to clear up the mess before Dad got back off the night shift.

I'm only sixteen and I've got dishpan hands, he thought, and laughed as he stacked the plates neatly on the draining-board. Who the hell cares anyway? Adrian-types with long, delicate fingers maybe. Not me. Helen might care, I suppose. I wonder if that's what she likes about him: his smooth hands. Mike scrubbed away at a fork. Smooth bloody everything, he thought, smooth voice, smooth clothes, altogether too smooth for his own good. I haven't got a snowflake's chance in a blast furnace with Helen while he's around. She doesn't even know I'm here. All the girls say he's beautiful, and I

63

suppose he is if you like that sort of thing, the long, thin, colourless type.

Mike ran down the road to the bus stop. Every school day was a good day. Helen was at school, wasn't she? And it was art on Monday. Adrian couldn't draw to save his life. That's one thing I can do and he can't, thought Mike. There might be some others, but I haven't found out what they are yet.

Fletcher Grange High School stood at the intersection of two main roads, a large, long, white building surrounded by playing fields, lawns, tennis courts, outbuildings and an intricate arrangement of gravel paths. The constant streams of traffic flowing past it gave it the appearance of an ocean liner in a sea full of tiny fish. It was the biggest comprehensive school in the area (purpose-built, as the Head never tired of saying), and every morning two thousand pupils streamed into its gates, navy blue and yellow waves breaking over the grassy slopes, spreading themselves through the corridors, filling up the empty rooms.

"Hey! Carol!" Adrian could see the red hair just in front of him. "Carol, hang on a sec, will you?"

Carol turned and, seeing him, smiled.

"Hi."

"Hello." People pushed past them, not looking where they were going, elbowing, crushing.

"Phew!" Adrian said. "Bloody first years! What are they in such a hurry for? Come over here, I want to tell you something."

Carol leaned against a radiator. She tossed her hair out of her eyes and looked down as Adrian approached.

"Carol, did you mean what you said on Saturday?"

"Yes. Yes, of course I did. You should know that."

"I do. I haven't been able to sleep or eat or anything. I feel — mad. Just not like my normal self at all. Really. Because of you."

Carol laughed. "I've been thinking about you a lot, too.

But what about Helen. Have you told her?''

"No. I haven't seen her. I'll tell her, though. I'll tell her today. I promise. Will you wait for me at three-thirty? I'll walk home with you.''

"Not if you don't tell her.''

"But I will, really.''

"That's O.K., then. I must go now. I'm late as it is.'' Carol waved at him as she swung along the corridor. How, thought Adrian, does she manage to look sexy in a pleated uniform skirt? He remembered what she was wearing at the disco on Saturday: a slippery, silver sort of dress that flowed around her body like oil.

"Hello, Adrian.''

"Oh. Hello Helen.''

"You were late today. I waited for you at the gate. Did you have a nice weekend?''

"Not bad,'' said Adrian and added: "What about you.''

"I missed you.''

"Yeah, I know. I had a hell of a lot of work.''

"I know. You told me.''

"Helen, listen. I can't talk now. Can I see you at break? There's something . . . I mean I want to talk to you about something. O.K.?''

"Yes, sure.''

"One of the music rooms. All right? Number Four. No one'll be there at break.''

"Does it have to be there? Why not outside?''

"It's private. Don't want the whole lot of them gawping. O.K.?''

"Yes. 'Bye.''

"See you, then?''

"'Bye.''

Helen frowned as she walked to her classroom. In all the months that she'd been going out with Adrian, he'd never once asked to talk to her like that, in that special way, during school time. Every kind of reason for it went through her

65

mind: the doctor had given him six months to live, his family was moving away from the area, he had been transferred to another school.

"Thought you were never coming," whispered her friend Rebecca. "Wherever have you been? Moony's in a foul temper. You can tell. Look at the way she's done her hair. She looks as if she stuck every hairpin in like a knife."

"I've been talking to Adrian," Helen whispered back. "I'm meeting him at break in one of the music rooms."

Rebecca closed her eyes and pretended to swoon.

"Love's young dream," she cooed.

"Stop that clowning, Rebecca Wood, and get your books out. Page 137. You may begin reading at the top of the page, Rebecca."

"Yes, Miss Moon," Rebecca sighed, and lifted her eyes to heaven as she opened her book.

Adrian was finding it difficult to concentrate. He frowned at his book and chewed the top of his pen and thought about break. And Helen. Perhaps, he thought, I'm ill. Perhaps it's not normal to feel like this. Maybe there's something wrong with me. Maybe I don't know what love is. After all, last week I was so sure I loved Helen, and now . . . after Carol on Saturday night . . . maybe that's not love either and I'll see someone else I'll like better. He shook his head. How were you supposed to tell, anyway? What was real love and what was just fancying? Was there such a thing as love? He looked around at all the others. They wouldn't know. Maybe love was just fancying someone and liking them a lot at the same time. But what if you fancied more than one person? That didn't seem to be allowed, somehow. You couldn't go out with two people. You had to pair up, like Noah's Ark animals. I wish I looked different, he thought miserably. Everyone thinks I'm an expert at all this stuff, and there's no one I can ask.

"Ah, Wheeler, I'm glad I bumped into you." Mr.

Rowbotham, the woodwork teacher, caught up with Mike. "Are you on the way to metalwork?"

"Yes, sir. I'm a bit late, sir."

"Never mind. You can say you were having a word with me. It's about those flats for the first act. Someone's made a right pig's ear of them, and that's a fact. Looks more like a cotton wool factory than a cherry orchard. Thing is, they'll have to be redone, and quite sharpish. Dress rehearsal tomorrow night. Can you stay after school? I'll press-gang some helpers for you, but I do want you there, Wheeler, since you're the only one who knows what's what. Right?"

"O.K., sir. I'll come to the workshop after school."

"Good. Thanks very much."

"That's all right," said Mike and tore along the corridor to his metalwork class, his rubber soles squeaking on the linoleum.

Damn, damn, damn and blast it, he thought. No chance of bumping into Helen accidentally on purpose at the bus stop now, is there? Bloody Monday morning. What a way to start the week.

"Helen, hi. Sorry I'm a bit late."

"That's O.K. Is anything the matter, Adrian? I've been so worried, honestly. I didn't take in one word of French. I've just been thinking about you."

"It's nothing to worry about really."

"Please tell me what it is then. I can't bear the suspense."

Adrian didn't answer. He stood looking at the floor, examining the toes of his shoes with an expression of deep concern on his face.

"If you don't tell me what's the matter," said Helen "I'll go crazy, Adrian. Please."

"O.K. I'll tell you then. It's just," said Adrian, "that I've fallen in love. With someone else, I mean. I never meant it to happen, and I never meant to hurt you, Helen, honestly I didn't, but it just kind of happened to me, and I thought I had to tell you, because I didn't want to . . . to cheat you and so on

67

and I'm really very fond of you, and I'm sorry. That's all."

All? A great, white scream rose up and filled Helen's mind. What did he mean, all? She felt as though someone had pushed her off the pleasant, grassy path on which she had been walking, and down a vast, black cliff-face. She felt that she was falling and falling, that her body would fly apart with a thousand hurting pieces at any moment. She said:

"Who is it?"

"It doesn't matter."

"Tell me. I want to know."

"It's Carol Philips."

Carol. The red head. That's that then, thought Helen. I'm not any kind of competition for her. She said: "She's older than you."

"Only one year. Anyway, it doesn't matter."

"No, I don't suppose it does."

"Are you O.K? Will you be O.K?"

She wanted to tear his hair out by the handful, scratch his smooth cheeks with her nails, beat her fists on his white shirt, and rip it apart.

"Sure. Why not?" she said, as lightly as she could. "Happens all the time, doesn't it?"

"You'll . . . find someone else, you know. You're terrific."

"Thank you," said Helen with dignity, "for those few kind words. Will you go now, please?"

"You'll be O.K? Promise?"

"Flatter yourself, don't you? What did you think I'd do, lie down and die? Forget it. Go back to what's her face and tell her she's bloody well welcome to you."

Adrian blushed. He took a tentative step towards Helen, stretched out his hand.

"Adrian," she said in a level voice that surprised her, "if you so much as lay one finger on me, I swear I'll tear you to pieces. Now just go, will you? Go."

He went.

"Have you told her, then?" Carol ran a hand casually

through her long hair.

"Yes."

"How did she take it?"

"How would you take it?"

"Me? I'd scratch out your eyes," she purred.

Adrian sighed. "Helen's not like that. She's nice."

"I get it," said Carol. "Having second thoughts, are you?"

"Don't be so bloody silly."

"What's up, then?"

"Nothing at all. Everything's fine."

"Come round to my house tonight. They're all off to the pictures or somewhere. I'll cheer you up." She lowered her long-lashed eyes demurely.

"Can't wait," Adrian whispered.

"See you at dinner, O.K?"

"O.K." Adrian walked towards his classroom with a lump in his throat that might have been anger, or regret, or sorrow. He thought doggedly of Carol so as to blot out the image of Helen's sad face that seemed to have become imprinted on his mind.

"Has anyone seen Helen Banks?" said Mr. Linton. Rebecca put up her hand.

"She . . . she wasn't feeling very well," she said, improvizing. "Before break. She's probably sitting down in one of the cloakrooms. Shall I go and see if I can find her?"

"Very well. And don't you get lost, please. Come straight back if you have no luck, otherwise you will find that meaty bits of Louis XIV's foreign policy have just passed you by."

Rebecca ran towards the music rooms. Stupid things, she thought, she'll only get into trouble, snogging at break, honestly. Can't they wait?

"Helen?" she called. "Helen, where are you?"

There was no answer. Rebecca looked in every one of the practice rooms. She found Helen in the last one of all, sitting on the floor with her head on her knees, crying as if she never

69

intended to stop.

"Oh my God, Helen," she said. "What's happened? Whatever's wrong?"

As Mike pushed his way into the canteen, Adrian and Carol were on their way out. Her arm was draped elegantly across his shoulders, and she was looking at him with eyes like headlights, as though she were starving and he were a cream cake. That's odd, Mike thought. Most peculiar. When did that happen? And did Helen know? Where was Helen, anyway? He looked round the enormous room for her. She was at a table by herself, with her back to him. Rebecca would be at the rehearsal of course. Helen's back was very straight and she seemed not to be eating. He sighed. Probably she had seen that exhibition Adrian and Carol were putting on for everyone's benefit. He went to collect his food.

"What's for dinner, then?"

"Stew." Slap, slap went spoonfuls of mashed swede and boiled spuds. Mike pulled a face at the food and took his plate over to Helen's table.

"Mind if I sit here?" he said, as gently as he could.

"Suit yourself." Helen didn't even look up.

"Food gets worse and worse, doesn't it?"

"I didn't notice."

"That's because you haven't eaten it."

"I don't want it."

"I'll take your plate away, then, shall I? Save you the trouble."

"Ta."

Mike took the plate back to the hatch.

"What's for afters?" he asked.

"Apple pie and custard."

"Give us some, then."

"You only just took your first course."

"It's for a friend."

Helen looked up as Mike came back carrying a plate of apple pie.

70

"You didn't have to get my pudding," she said, hearing how silly she sounded, like a spoilt child.

"Well," Mike sat down and began to eat. "I reckon you should have something. Make you feel better."

"Nothing could."

Helen felt his eyes on her and looked up. Immediately, she looked away, fighting back tears.

"My sister's like that," he said placidly. "Goes off her food if something's not right."

Helen said nothing.

Mike continued: "I've only got the one sister. Three brothers, though. Proper little devils they are. I've got my hands full, I can tell you."

"What about your Mum?" Helen asked. In spite of herself, she was interested in the idea of Mike, ordinary Mike, looking after all those children. One hour alone with Kathy was enough to send her up the wall.

"Mum works the day shift, Dad works the night shift and I fill up all the gaps. And," he added, "I'm a damn good cook. A lot better than they've got here."

Helen smiled.

"That's better," said Mike. He sat and looked at her, not knowing what to say next. He wanted to throw his arms around her and stroke her hair and say, "It doesn't matter, really. I'll look after you. I'll love you. I won't leave you, not ever." But you couldn't say things like that in the middle of the canteen. Not without some kind of lead-up.

"Be late home tonight," he said, in the end. "Got to stay behind and repaint some flats in the workshop. Rowbotham says the third years have made the Cherry Orchard look like a cotton-wool factory." He waited for her smile, but she was staring at the plate.

"Look," he whispered, leaning towards her. "I know you're hurting."

"Do you?" Helen spoke angrily. "How do you know? And do you know how much?"

"I reckon."

"Well, you don't. No one does."

"O.K. Forget it."

"No, I'm sorry." Helen smiled at him. "I didn't mean to bite your head off. It's just that . . ."

"Don't worry. I know. It's O.K."

"I've got to get back to the classroom."

"Hang on. Wait for me. I'll come with you."

They walked without speaking down crowded corridors. At the door of their classroom, Mike put his hand gently on her arm.

"Helen?"

"Yes?"

"Fancy staying on at three-thirty and helping me paint?"

Helen was just about to say no, when she met his eyes. She was surprised by the intensity of feeling on his face. He really wanted her to stay and paint. It mattered to him. She looked down at his hand on her arm, a square, brown hand with strong, short fingers, slightly stained with paint.

"O.K.," she said. "Got nothing better to do."

"It'll be fun, you'll see." He grinned. "Nothing like laying on thick dollops of paint for making a person feel better. I'll meet you at the workshop."

"Right. See you, then."

"See you."

I've done it now, Mike thought. There's no going back, even if I wanted to, which I don't. I won't be able to talk much in the workshop, what with everyone around and all those cherry trees to fix, but I'll ask her out after, for a coffee or something. She'll probably say no. I mean, after what's happened with Adrian, she'll want to go home, most likely. And if she does come, I won't think anything of it, Mike warned himself. I won't take it as meaning too much. He sighed. The best he could hope for was to see Helen a bit while she was on the rebound . . . but maybe . . . Mike blushed, thinking of all those stories in his Mum's magazines which he read secretly sometimes, as though they were dangerous and shameful

72

drugs. In those stories, the girl always discovered that the handsome, flashy character was no good at all, and the plain boy-next-door was really the one for her, and quite handsome, too, if you looked at him properly. Load of garbage, those stories. Everyone knew that. But his hands were trembling as he put them back in his pockets, and a thick feeling rose up in his throat whenever he thought of Helen, which seemed to be nearly all the time. The clock was going round so slowly. Come on, home-time. Get a move on.

Mike said: "Do you see what they've done? They've made all the little white blobs round and symmetrical. It really does look like a window at Christmas. We've got to try and get it looking much more kind of misty, cloudy. Know what I mean?"

"Yes, I do," Helen said, "but I don't know how you're going to do it. I certainly couldn't. Isn't there anything easier for me?"

"Sure. You can start up there on the sky. It's not the right colour. Too blue. Slosh on a bit of this, and that should do it. O.K?"

"Yes. Fine."

They worked together without speaking. Someone had brought a radio, and the sound of The Police filled the air. A few children were assembling all the props on a table over by the far wall. Mr. Rowbotham, oblivious to the radio, was humming snatches from *The Mikado* as he hammered a rather shaky-looking door into its frame. For the first time since he had told her about Carol, Helen found that she could think about Adrian with something like calm. Perhaps it was the painting after all, just as Mike had said: smooth blue-grey sticky swatches of it, sliding off the end of her brush. She looked up at Mike. He was working quickly, efficiently, and without, it seemed, taking any notice of her at all. And all the little blobs that had looked like cotton wool became, as he touched them, bunches of cherry blossom, tinged with pink, so real that you could almost smell them, almost imagine

73

yourself out of this noisy workshop and walking between trees at dawn. What about when it's over, Helen wondered. I shall have to go home then, and tell Mum, and Kathy will be unbearable and . . . she nearly started crying all over again.

"I could do with a Coke," said Mike. "Sweaty work, this is."

"Yes. Me, too." Back and forth across the canvas went Helen's brush. She didn't look up.

"Have you got time to come to the Rex, after? Just for a Coke?"

"O.K." Helen said. "But I can't be too late."

"Great!" Mike smiled at her. He looks nice when he smiles, Helen thought. Not beautiful, like Adrian. No one could call him that, but nice. Safe and solid, like brown bread and butter. She smiled back.

"Super," Mike added, "to see you smiling, I mean."

"I do sometimes, you know."

"Not a lot today, though. That's what I meant."

"No, not today. I'm sorry if I was a bit . . . you know, a bit off at dinner-time."

"That's O.K." Mike nodded. "Nearly done now. How about you?"

"Just this corner."

They worked in silence for the next ten minutes, then Mike said: "Right. Let's get Rowbotham to check this, then we can go."

"I'll just go and wash my hands and get my stuff. See you outside."

As she walked out of the workshop, she looked back at the flat they had been painting. Mike was holding it up for Mr. Rowbotham to see. It looked exactly like an orchard in the spring time, and her piece of sky looked quite reasonable too.

"You've been going out with him for ages, haven't you?" Mike had finished his Coke in three large gulps and now sat turning the glass around in his hands.

"Almost a year. We've never been in the same class or

74

anything, but we saw quite a lot of each other in the Christmas concert last year and then, well, it sort of started with that.''

''Not like us,'' Mike smiled. ''We've been in the same class since the First Year. Bet you never even noticed I was there for the first three years.''

''I did. You were always getting into trouble then.''

''Ah, but I'm a reformed character now, aren't I?''

''I suppose so,'' Helen sighed. ''Do you know, I feel as if I've been asleep. Don't you think that's funny? When I was . . . I mean, when we . . . Adrian and me were going out and all that, I just didn't notice anything else. Isn't that awful? I've just given the whole of life a miss for nearly a year, all because of bloody Adrian. Can you believe that? There are people in the class I don't remember having seen for months.''

''That's love,'' Mike said. '' 'A bright stain on the vision, blotting out reason.' ''

''That's great! Did you think of that?''

''Don't be daft. That's Robert Graves. He also calls love 'the universal migraine'.''

''That's right. That's just exactly right.'' Helen looked pleased. ''I wish they could give you an aspirin or something for it, though. I didn't know you liked poetry.''

''There's plenty of stuff about me you don't know,'' Mike said gently. ''For one thing, I know all about your old friend, Love.''

''Really? Are you in love? Tell me.''

''Yes, of course. Doesn't it show?''

''No, if you want to know the truth. I'd never have guessed.''

''I'm the strong, silent type. None of your old wearing your-heart-on-your-sleeve junk for me. Besides, it's unrequited.''

''Who is it? You can tell me. I bet you're just shy. Maybe if you told me, I could kind of suss her out. See what she thinks, you know.''

"Would you?"

"Sure."

"O.K., then. I'll tell you."

"Go on then, what're you waiting for?"

"It's embarrassing, that's what."

"Oh, go on. I won't laugh. Promise."

"It's you."

"Me?"

"Yes."

"You're kidding."

"No."

"Truly?"

"Truly."

Helen said, after some thought: "I think you're just saying that to cheer me up. It's very kind of you, but it won't work. You really shouldn't use yourself as an aspirin for my general migraine, or whatever you called it."

"Universal migraine," Mike said quietly, "and I'm not."

"Not what?"

"Not saying it to cheer you up. Every day when I get up, I can't wait to get to school, just to see you. Every day I don't manage to catch the same bus home as you do, I'm fed up the whole evening. It's true. It's probably the worst time in the world to tell you, but there you are. I've done it now. Have you finished your Coke? We'd better get home."

"Yes. All right." Helen pulled on her jacket and walked quickly towards the door, not wanting to look at Mike. Could it be true? All those months, seeing her with Adrian. How it must have hurt him. Mind, he'd cashed in on the situation pretty damn quickly, stepping in and being nice to her almost before she had dried her eyes, trying to get her on the rebound. I'd do the same, though, she thought, so I'm a fine one to talk. If Adrian were . . . deserted like that, I'd rush to comfort him.

"You don't have to walk all the way home with me, you know," she said.

"I want to."

"Quite the gentleman!"

"Got nothing to do with it."

"Why then? I'll be O.K. on my own."

"I just want to, that's all."

"But why?"

"Need a bloody essay on the subject, do you?" Mike sounded really angry now. "Because I want to be with you, looking at you every minute I possibly can. Get it?"

"Yes, and there's no need to shout."

Mike said nothing for a few minutes. That's it, thought Helen. He'll never speak to me again. Then: "I'm sorry I yelled at you," he said, looking away from her. "Really. I just want you to understand, that's all."

"I know. I'm sorry too. I still feel a bit peculiar."

"O.K." They had reached Helen's gate.

"I've got to go now. Thanks for the Coke and everything."

"Are you staying for the dress rehearsal tomorrow?"

"I've got nothing to do, though, have I?"

"You could help me, if you like. We could get some fish and chips after. On the way home." He seemed worried.

"O.K.," she said.

"Great. Terrific. I'll see you then." He turned to go, and then seemed to change his mind, and looked back at Helen. He's wondering if he can kiss me, she thought.

" 'Bye then," he said, and ran away without looking back.

Helen stood by the gate for a few moments, thinking, deliberately thinking about Adrian, testing how much it hurt her. To her amazement, she found these thoughts constantly interrupted by, it seemed, a quite different section of her mind wondering what Mike's kiss would have felt like. Am I plain fickle, she thought desperately. Am I?

"Had a good day, love?" asked her mother.

"Awful. I'm in a total muddle. I've got a headache."

"Go and take a couple of Aspirins, then. You know where they are."

6. *The Whole Truth*

October 10th, 1953

My name is James Morten. I am seventeen years old. I'm in the Sixth Form at a minor public school whose name doesn't matter. I've been at boarding-school since I was eight because my parents live abroad. In North Borneo, to be precise. A town called Jesselton. I was born there. During the War, we were kept, my mother and I, in a Japanese prison camp, which wasn't much fun at the time, but won me an awestruck admiration from the other boys when I first went to school. I was thought of as rather gallant and dashing, and I played on this for a long time, emphasizing the cruelty and hardship aspects of the camp, and skating over the boredom and hunger, which were what I chiefly remembered. Boredom and hunger, after all, are an integral part of life at any school.

During the Christmas and Easter holidays for as long as I can remember, I've been going to assorted relatives and friends, but in the long, summer months I've always gone home. To Jesselton. That's how I think of it: as my home, even though I only see it for a short time every year. When I'm at school in England, I miss the place rather than my parents. It wasn't always like that. I used to miss my mother and father dreadfully when I was younger, and now I feel a certain amount of guilt that I need them so little, think of them so seldom. For the last couple of years, my thoughts have been full of Anne.

A few words about Anne. I have known her almost all my life. We were always friends. She lived in Jesselton and didn't come back to school in England because her mother is a teacher and educated Anne at home in what seemed to me a

78

rather rough and ready fashion. For about a year, since the summer before last, in fact, I had been writing to her and she to me and, because of the distance and something else I haven't been able to put my finger on (maybe a need for excitement), the letters had become more and more sentimental, more and more loving, more and more like proper love letters. I used to get teased about it quite a lot. Last term, all through the Coronation festivities, all through the exams, I longed for the holidays when I would see her. I felt a little shy: all those things we had written — would I be able to translate them into physical action, into real, spoken words? It's all very well to sit in your study and write things like: ''I long to put my arms around you'' (and that was relatively tame, I can tell you. I used to get a bit carried away during prep. on long, summer evenings) and quite another to go up to a girl, even one I had known for years and actually *do* such a thing. So I think that you could say that I arrived in Jesselton in a mood of pleasurable anticipation.

I had photographs of Anne, naturally, and I'd stared at them for a whole year, but they weren't very good. She seemed always to be squinting into the sun, or shielding her face with her hand, or hidden by a straw hat or something. Still, I thought I had a fairly decent image of her lodged permanently in my mind. I wasn't prepared for what had happened to her in the year since I had last seen her. She had grown up. I suppose I had, too, but you don't notice it so much in yourself. I was still ordinary-looking. Dark hair, brown eyes, straight nose, not too short. Not bad, but not a matinee idol or anything. Anne had always been pretty. My parents, everyone, had been saying it since she was four. A pretty little girl. She came to see me the first night I was home, and we sat on the verandah, rather tongue-tied after such a long time, saying stupid things like: ''Did you have a good trip?'' (Anne) and ''I'd forgotten quite how hot it is'' (me), and I stared and stared at her. She had become beautiful.

Beauty: now there's a poser for any would-be writer! How do you get it down, fix it? A painter can show it, but what can

I do? Give you the individual features, gentle reader, and let you get on with it? It's very hard. Your blue-eyed long-legged blonde won't be Anne, won't be anything like her. You'll imagine your own. I can't put down exactly what she was like, only words that summon her to *my* mind, and this worries me, but it doesn't really matter, since I know what she looked like, and this is being written just for me anyway. So I can say whatever I want to say. She was like a gazelle. Her hair was the colour of sand, flat and smooth around her head. Her eyes were huge and set very far apart and their colour changed every time I saw her. I'll put down ''pale grey eyes'' and that should cover it. Her fingers were very long and slim, and her mouth really was like a rosebud. It's quite easy to see where clichés come from. They're very often no more or less than the exact truth. Her mouth was like a rosebud — take it or leave it. She was always quiet, which I liked because it gave me a chance to talk without interruption. She was the ideal audience. I talked and talked that night, I remember, about all sorts of things. We arranged to go swimming the next day. She left in the end without any more than a brotherly hand-shake on my part. Well, my parents were there too. Even Casanova couldn't have done more in the circumstances.

We met on the beach early next morning before it got too hot. Places are a little easier to describe than people. You can say: the sea was like blue glass, the sand like fine powder, and Bob's your uncle. We ran into the warm waves like little children, and swam and did duck dives and looked at the strangely corrugated sand under the water, and kept an eye open for jellyfish and pointed shells and silver fishes in the groves of coral that cropped up here and there along the sea bed. Anne was a good swimmer. We raced and splashed and it was quite easy and natural during one of these rowdy skirmishes simply to slip an arm through the water and put it around her waist. Easy, but I was nervous, I remember. Her face was suddenly very close to mine.

''Anne,'' I said. ''Anne.'' My head seemed to have emptied itself of words.

"Do you want to kiss me?"

"Yes. Yes, I do."

She closed her eyes and put her arms around my neck and I kissed her. Her lips tasted soft and salty. We were out of our depth in the sea, and I suppose we forgot to tread water in the excitement of the moment and the next thing I knew, we were both submerged and choking and spluttering as we pushed our way back to the surface. Later, on the beach, we managed a bit better. We kissed properly. I stroked her arms and her back. I held her close to me. I took her hand as we walked to my house for breakfast, and didn't let go until we got to the verandah steps. As I kissed her there (quickly, in case my parents were looking), I was lulled, and calm. It was like falling asleep after a stormy night at sea. It was, I assumed at the time, perfect love.

That same evening, my parents played bridge with some people called Constantine. I had never met them before. They were new to the Colony, but my mother told me as much as she knew about them in advance.

"He's much older than she is. He's Greek originally, I think. No one seems to know that much about them, but you know your father. He'd play cards with the Devil himself, if he thought it would be a good game. She's called Poppy. Some people say she's Portuguese. Or maybe Greek too. In any case, she doesn't seem to go about much. One hardly ever sees her. She's quite strange, actually, but they're both fiendishly good bridge players. Daddy and I will have to look to our laurels."

It was true. Mrs. Constantine was strange. I watched her shuffling the cards that night, and couldn't decide if she was beautiful or hideous. If Anne reminded me of a gazelle, then Mrs. Constantine was like a snake: supple and seemingly without bones, smooth, lustrous, with wicked black eyes like stones and shining black hair twisted up into a knot on top of her head and a wide, wide mouth with disturbingly red lips and a flickering tongue that darted out to lick the crimson lips when she was concentrating on the cards. I was mesmerized by that mouth, by the sharp edges of white teeth I could see when she smiled. I sat in an armchair with a copy of *Punch* and pretended to read it, but my eyes kept going back to those lips and that tiny corner of pink tongue and I was in a turmoil. My stomach felt as if a huge wheel lurched and turned inside it every time she moved. My hands felt weak. I could hardly turn the pages of my magazine. In the end, I couldn't stand it any longer. I went out on to the verandah for some air. A little while later, someone opened the door and stepped out behind me. I knew from the thick fragrance that filled the air that it was Mrs. Constantine. I turned round. She stood there, shrugging her shoulders.

"I am dummy," she said, "so I've come to talk to you. Better than breathing down my poor husband's neck, willing him to make tricks, don't you think?"

"Oh, undoubtedly," I answered. She was wearing a tight sort of dress in shiny, slippery silk, which looked as if it had been painted on to her body. She seemed to have nothing on underneath, which made the wheel in my stomach behave in an entirely crazy fashion. How did I know she had nothing on under her dress? Well, in fact I didn't know, not for certain, but I couldn't see any signs at all of brassière straps or elastic waistbands which I hadn't been able to help noticing on all other women.

She talked to me for what seemed a very long time. It must have been a difficult hand poor Mr. Constantine was playing. She made me talk. She listened in such a way as to make every remark of mine appear the last word in wit. She flashed her teeth at me. She offered me a cigarette. She let me light her cigarette. She asked me to call her "Poppy". She teased me. She ruffled my hair. She stood very close to me, leaning on the verandah railings, so that I could feel, or imagined I could feel, the warmth of her skin. Then they started calling her back to the bridge game. I'm sure, rationally, that what happened next actually *did* happen, but when I write it down, even now after all this time, it seems so amazing to me that I can hardly believe it was true. At times I think perhaps I imagined it, wished it so much that now it seems real, but it wasn't like that. It really did happen. Right there, only feet away from where my parents and her husband were sitting.

"I'm coming," she called back to the card players, over her shoulder, and then she put a silky arm round my neck and drew my face down to hers, and fastened those red, red lips on to my mouth and darted her snake-like tongue between my teeth and pressed her whole soft body right up to mine and seemed to squirm with pleasure. I nearly fainted.

"I will see you again," she whispered. "Lovely, lovely boy." And then she was gone leaving me shaking with every turbulent feeling you can think of.

I didn't sleep much that night. I lay in the small, gauzy tent made by my mosquito net and tossed and turned and had one dream after another. Most of the dreams were about Anne, I think. At least, the bits that I recalled in the morning were about Anne, but behind the dreams, somewhere at the edges of my mind, an image of Poppy seemed to be lurking.

Gradually, over the next few days, I forgot all about the night of the bridge party. Perhaps it would be truer to say that other things that I was doing made it seem less important. I think of that week as the time before everything went mad. It was my happiest time with Anne. We were together all the time: played languid games of tennis on the court behind her house, swam, went on picnics, went for long walks up the lower slopes of Kinabalu, the mountain whose green and mauve shadowed mass loomed over Jesselton. We sat in the Club drinking iced drinks and listening to talk of England, we went to dinner with various people — the Wentworths, the James', the Winters — we did all the things that we were used to doing. But it was a magical time because running through everything like a fine, golden thread was the knowledge that we loved one another. Whenever I could, whenever we were alone, I would kiss her, and I used to hold her hand as much as possible, even in public. Sometimes I would catch her looking at me with such intensity of feeling that my breath left me for a moment. I loved her, I'm sure of that. I would have sworn at that time that I loved her as much as she did me, more even, but subsequent events proved me wrong.

Our week of innocent pleasure ended on Saturday night at the Club dance. Anne and I were there together. Everyone was there. All the ladies had put on their best floral evening frocks, the flags left over from the Coronation came into their own again, the fairy lights were lit on the verandah, and the gramophone churned out all the old favourites: "Jealous Heart", "Pawnshop on the Corner", "Tennessee Waltz", and lots of Glenn Miller. Anne and I danced. We made small talk to everyone we knew and I drank rather a lot of gin and ginger ale. Perhaps I can blame it all on the gin (please, I was drunk, I didn't know what I was doing, it wasn't my fault, etc.) but I doubt it. I felt perfectly normal. I remember everything that happened. Doesn't that mean that I was at least a little sober?

It happened when I was standing beside Anne, resting between dances. Something made me glance over to the long french windows leading to the back verandah, and there she was: Poppy, dressed from head to foot in black. She seemed to be melting into the darkness behind her. Only her red mouth glowed, and even from across the room I could see it smiling straight at me, the lips shining in the light as though she had just licked them, as though they were still moist. She saw me looking at her and beckoned me, crooking her finger and inclining her head backwards, indicating the verandah. If only — useless words. If only my father had not chosen that very moment to ask Anne to dance, then what? I don't know. I really don't know. But he did, and off she went and I was left alone. My legs were trembling. I put my glass down on the nearest table and made my way out of the room. I think it was in my mind to ask Poppy to dance, to bring her into the lighted room and behave perfectly normally. After all, she was an acquaintance of my parents.

"Mrs. Constantine," I whispered into the night.

"I'm here," said a voice from a little way away. "Come down here and find me."

"But it's so dark."

"I'll help you. I'll guide you."

I went down the steps. The slope of a hill stretches down to the playing fields. There are oleander bushes and flame of the forest trees. I began to look for her.

"Here I am," she said suddenly. "You've found me."

"Yes," I said foolishly. "Can I get you a drink? Or perhaps you would like to come in and dance."

She laughed. "There's only one thing I'd like to do, beloved, and that's eat you alive. Do you know that I eat little boys like you for breakfast?" I giggled nervously. What a peculiar person she was. I'd never heard any of my mother's friends talk like that. Even her voice, detached from the funny things she said, was like honey and gravel stones all mixed up.

"I'd be a bit of a knobbly mouthful," I ventured, trying to keep things light, feeling even then that this talk was closing over my head like water and likely to drown me.

"Not at all," she whispered, "tasty and sweet and smooth." And before I could speak she was all over me. Now I've seen that written before and never quite believed it, but I swear that was what was happening. Her mouth was everywhere, biting me and sucking my mouth and kissing me, and her fingers pinched and stroked and her legs coiled round my legs until every bit of me was throbbing and burning and twitching and I was only conscious of never wanting it to stop. From far away I heard voices (Anne's voice, said part of my mind . . . stop, that's Anne's voice) but I was too far gone. My eyes were closed, and that tongue, oh that tongue tasted so sweet! After minutes, hours, Poppy drew away, leaving my nerve ends raw and shrieking far more.

"You see," she said, "you can't stop me. Nothing can stop me. If I want to gobble you up, lovely boy, then gobble you up I shall."

She smiled at me and in the dark her mouth seemed covered in blood, and looking at her, I felt sick, disgusted with her, with myself, with everything. I ran all the way back up the slope and into the lighted lounge. I saw Anne before she saw me. She looked pale and insubstantial, like a ghost, as though she had faded while I was with Poppy.

"James, where have you been?" she said. "You look dreadful. Are you all right?"

Oh, God, I thought, she can see the lipstick all over me. I blushed. "Just a bit the worse for gin," I said.

Anne looked at me and I could see, even in the state I was in, that there were tears in her eyes.

"You look so funny. Different. What shall I do if you're different? It will be like being with somebody else. I want you just as you are."

"I'll be all right, really. In a few minutes. I'll just go and fix myself up."

In the lavatory I stared at the mirror. There was no lipstick anywhere, not on my skin, nor on my clothes. But Poppy had . . . I felt faint as I remembered all the things that mouth had done, and I sat down quickly, touching my burning face. Why hadn't her lipstick come off? It was impossible. My mind felt fuzzy. Perhaps after all I was drunk? I put my head under the tap and let the cool water run over me. Anne must have wondered where I'd got to, I thought. She must have been worried. I said these things to myself and I didn't care. Quite suddenly whether Anne worried or what she thought were not of the least importance. I was light-headed, even after I'd dried my face. My veins seemed full of a fiery substance that burned its way round my body. Poppy's mouth had infected me with a disease of wanting and that was all I knew. I wanted to see her again. I wanted her. There didn't seem to be any space in my head for Anne at all.

I didn't say anything about this, naturally. Everything went on as normal and I tried to be as pleasant as I could and as loving towards Anne as I had always been, but she must have noticed that a part of me was absent: simply somewhere else. Now I realize I should have told her, should have explained, talked it out with her, but it's easy to be clever afterwards. She never showed that she was hurt or angry or jealous or anything. I never saw any signs in her eyes, but then again, maybe I wasn't looking.

About ten days after the Club dance, my mother and father and I, and Anne and her parents drove up to spend a few days in the Rest House at Kota Belud, a beauty spot on the upper slopes of Kinabalu. The drive is spectacular: gorges and tropical rain forests and waterfalls on every hand, but I thought only of Poppy. I hadn't seen her since that night at the Club and I was beginning to despair of ever seeing her again.

Have you guessed? She was staying at the Rest House.

''Alone,'' she told my mother on the first night. ''My poor husband. Always the business.''

She sat by herself in the dining room and looked at me over Anne's head.

There wasn't much to do at Kota Belud. We rode a little, walked, talked, played cards in the evening and I looked out for Poppy. I never saw her in the daytime. I don't know where she went or what she did, but at night she was always there, curled up on the rattan chaise-longue, looking at me.

There was a bridge at Kota Belud, made of string and matchsticks, it seemed to me, suspended from one side of the river to the other. When you walked along it, it swung from side to side in a most terrifying fashion. Below it, the greenish water foamed over rocks and there were alligators lurking in the stony caves along the bank. So people said. Anne refused to put one foot on this bridge.

''But what if we want to have a picnic on the other side?'' I asked.

''There's nothing wrong with this side,'' she answered. ''I wouldn't be seen dead on that bridge.''

''Not even for me?''

''No,'' she said, and that was that.

Poppy, it seems clear to me now, bided her time until our last night. I suppose that was kind of her in a funny sort of way. My parents and Anne's parents and Anne could so easily have had their holiday destroyed from the very beginning.

After dinner on our last night, then, while Anne was pouring coffee at the sideboard, Poppy walked behind my chair and whispered in my ear.

"Tonight," she said. "Leave your door open and wait."

I watched the hands of the clock going round the whole evening. My heart was racing and my knees shook uncontrollably. My mouth was dry and I was sweating.

"I hope you're not coming down with a fever, dear," said my mother. I've got the fever, I wanted to say. I'm sick unto death. I'm dying for her. It's too late. At last, the time came and everyone went to bed. The Rest House was silent. Only the darkness outside was full of noises: insects and the frothing of the river in the deep gorge and the creaking of old wood.

I lay under my mosquito net and waited. I think I must have slept a little. I don't remember hearing Poppy come into the room. Before I knew it, she was lying beside me in the small white tent. She was naked. Perhaps she had slipped something into my coffee as she passed my chair — I don't know. Perhaps I really was sick. What I remember of that night resembles the memory of a dream: limbs twined round my own, and a loud, throbbing pounding noise that is my heart drumming in my ears, and a huge mouth like a scarlet flower fastened on to my mouth and my neck and my ears, and hands coiling around me and an immense and powerful heat spreading all over my body. I only remember one thing that she said and I don't know when she said it:

"I saw your little friend as I came here," she whispered in my ear. "It's late for a girl her age to be awake."

Then I slept as I have never slept before or since, a deep, drugged sleep like an anaesthetic.

When I woke up, it was dawn. Bit by bit, memories of the night came back to me. I lay in bed grinning with satisfaction, feeling elated, grown-up and full of energy. I thought of Poppy and was surprised to find that the fever that had raged in my blood since I had first seen her wasn't there any more. I felt peculiar. It was as though a pain that had been worrying me had disappeared. Anne, I thought at once. Oh, Anne, how terrible I've been to you! Quite suddenly, love for her, for gentle, golden Anne, flooded me, and I jumped out of bed, pushing back the net, wanting to run to her and tell her everything, wanting to confess and have her forgive me and kiss me with those soft, childish, soothing kisses. My door was open, and I was halfway across the room when I saw the snake curled just outside, as if in wait for me. I froze, and thought quickly. Was there anything at all that I could kill it with? I groped behind me for the chair. If I hit it with the chair-back ... I never had to. The snake lifted its head, looked at me out of small, black eyes like stones, flicked its tongue a couple of times, slithered to the edge of the verandah and disappeared. I sat on the bed for a few moments, recovering. Then I went to look for Anne. I went to tell her that I loved her. Only her. Forever.

She wasn't in her room. She wasn't anywhere. We looked and looked. A waiter from the Rest House found her body in the end, wedged between two rocks a little way downstream from the swinging bridge.

I don't need to dwell on the journey back to Jesselton, or her funeral or the hours of anguished talk about what everybody was calling "the accident". They all agreed that she fell off the bridge. They thought she may have been sleepwalking. Apparently as a child she used to do it quite often. But I know. I haven't ever said anything, but I know. Nothing in the world would have made her set foot on that bridge. Nothing but despair. Poppy's words keep coming back to me: "I saw your little friend as I came here ..." Anne had seen her going into my room, and she hadn't been able to bear it.

There you are, the long and the short of it. I killed her as surely as if I had stabbed her with a knife, shot her with a gun, squeezed her neck between my hands. Has there ever been a murderer in the Classical Sixth before?

Poppy? Well, Poppy vanished without trace. She ate me for breakfast and simply disappeared. I have my own theory, of course, but there's no need for me to add the title of "Lunatic" to that of "Murderer" is there? What the hell, though, while I'm about it — the whole truth. I think she turned into the snake outside my door that morning. I think, actually, that she was always a snake during the daylight hours, which is why I never saw her except at night. Then, she became Poppy and sought out new, tasty morsels. That's it. The end of the story. Now you can send for the ambulance, send for the straitjacket, send for the little men in white coats.

7. Alice

Alice. Alice would soon be home. It was nearly six o'clock. They were waiting for her in the old house: Louise, her mother, her aunt Bella and her grandmother, Irena. They did not pause in what they were doing, but all three of them knew, by the colour of the sky, by the beginnings of an unmistakeable pull around their hearts, that Alice had been gone long enough and would — must — soon be home again.

She came out of Miss Lucchesi's gate holding her violin case as if it were a weapon. Ben stopped in front of her.

"It's Alice, isn't it?" he said.

"Yes, that's right."

"I'm Ben Ackworth."

"I know. Miss Lucchesi told me."

"May I walk a little way with you?"

Alice looked down the road and then back to Miss Lucchesi's door with something like panic in her eyes.

"Yes," she said at last. "If you like."

As they walked together, Ben looked at Alice, and she stared with great concentration at the cracks in the pavement.

The upper floors of the house were no longer used. Neighbours looked up at the dark windows at night and wondered what could be hidden there, under dust sheets. Louise was standing in what used to be the studio long ago, when Irena still taught ballet. The room was empty, with a high ceiling and cold in the special icy, musty-smelling way of places that have known no heat for a long time. Oh, I remember them, thought Louise, the cold, blue hands of the dancers in the winter, their poor fragile necks and thin legs! A vast mirror still covered the whole of one wall. The glass was spotted and discoloured now, and in its depths Louise saw only a sepia-tinted reproduction of herself and of the room behind her. They had stood in front of it, all the girls, dancing: bending, stretching, making small movements of their hands and feet, gestures running into one another, perpetual motion bounded by a gilded frame carved into leaves and fruit and tiny coronets, all blackened now by age and by neglect.

She's up there now, thought Bella, up in that freezing studio, killing time till the child comes home, mooning, dreaming, turning disjointed thoughts over in her head, and we'll pay for it. It won't be long before she catches a chill, and then I'll really have my hands full. Bella shook her head as she had shaken it since childhood when she thought about her sister's foolishness in almost everything. She has mismanaged her life, Bella said to herself, walked through it dreaming. It was typical of everything Louise was that she should have thrown herself away on that dreadful Randall. Couldn't she see? By his hard eyes, and set mouth, by the way he spoke, that he was a cruel man? And as for the drinking, that should have been obvious to anyone. But at least he had been wealthy, and they would not have survived without his money, that was certain. Bella had to admit that Louise had a kind of courage. Or obstinacy. She had tried to hide everything, to keep it to herself, but her sister could tell, and Irena, too. They saw, couldn't help seeing, the eyes shadowed by nights of sleeplessness, reddened by tears. Bella was of the opinion that Randall had done them all an immense favour by dying when he did, but Louise regarded it as the greatest of all his cruelties.

Amazingly, she had loved him. And she had Alice. They all had Alice, of course, but Louise was the mother. I, Bella laughed, I'm just the aunt, the one who sees lessons are done, the one who teaches and organizes and cooks and mends and deals with the practical side of life. Bossy Bella. But someone has to do it, or the whole house would crumble around us. Bella was spreading plants and flowers out on a sheet of news-paper to dry: rose petals gathered at the end of the summer, stock and rosemary and lemon verbena, pinks and thyme and honeysuckle, bay leaves and mint. She was making pot-pourri as she did each year, to fill the bowls in all the rooms. Irena loved the fragrance, and Bella used to like it as a child, but now it filled her nostrils with the smoky smell of decay, of things drying up and dying. The whole house smelled of it, of lost youth shrivelled up into a kind of dust.

Bella is making pot-pourri, Irena thought, and Louise, who knows what she is doing? Floating somewhere. Not for the first time, Irena felt dissatisfied with her children. Louise did nothing, it seemed, and Bella never stopped working. She occupies herself all day, the old woman decided, so that she will not have time to think. She should have married. Some-one should have seen what a good wife she would have made. Clever, educated, efficient, but oh, how shy, how awkward with her body even as a child. I remember teaching her some dance steps in front of the mirror in the studio, standing next to her, showing her. What was she? Five? Or six? She tried. Bella always tries, but after a few minutes she burst into tears and would never go near that room again. I look wrong, she had said. Irena sighed. And I looked right, that was the trouble. Bella blames me because she has inherited nothing from me. There is no part of her face or body that resembles mine. Bella is like her father: thin, dark and angular. I will never, ever forgive him, for leaving me alone with two small girls in this enormous house. For running away.

Irena looked at the light fading outside the window. Louise had been like Alice once, and now she wandered round the house like a wraith, her mind never at rest. Surely Alice should be home soon? She folded her still-beautiful hands in her lap and said aloud: "O God, please keep the child from harm, from being hurt.''

She did not specify, even to herself, the harm that might
come to Alice, but it was bound up with love, with loving a
man. Alice was of an age when that kind of thing was a
danger. Irena regarded love as a disease, and moreover a
deceptive one. It filled you with glory for a time, but the glory
soon departed and then it left upon your spirit, oh, the most
appalling ravages.

Alice. He had never met anyone like her before. She
seemed foreign — not foreign to the place but a stranger to
the times she lived in.

He said: ''Will you let me walk home with you next
week?'' and added, because she hesitated: ''Please. I'd like to
know you better. To talk to you.''

The sun had set, and bands of light the colour of opals
streaked the edges of the sky. Her hair, he thought, is like a
cloud, like a pale mist around her shoulders.

''Maybe,'' she answered at last. ''But you must go now.
Please. They look out of the windows when it's time for me to
come home. Please. They wouldn't understand. They'd
think,'' she shook her head, ''I don't know what they'd
think. But they'd be worried and upset.''

''Who?'' he asked. ''Who would be upset?''

''My mother, and my aunt Bella and my grandmother.''

''But they must let you speak to your friends, surely?
There's nothing wrong with that.''

''I haven't any friends. They . . . oh, I can't explain. I
must go. Please let me.''

''But next week. Will you let me walk home with you?''

''Maybe.''

She was gone, through the tall wrought-iron gates into the
shadows of a rhododendron hedge that hid the lower part of
the house. Next week, Ben thought, she will come out for her
violin lesson, and I'll be here. I'll wait for her and walk with
her all the way to Miss Lucchesi's. He stood on the pavement
watching for something, some sign of her presence in the

house.

Louise heard the front door close and thought: Alice is home. She felt tension leaving her body. She smiled into the old mirror and tucked a strand of hair into the loose bun that she wore. Then she drifted out of the door and down the stairs, leaving the studio door open behind her.

She's back, thought Bella. I must heat the soup. Perhaps we could allow ourselves a small sherry before dinner just for a change. She took off her apron and went upstairs from the basement to suggest the extravagance to Irena. And to see the child.

They sat sipping their drinks, and because Irena was talking, her daughters were silent.

"You are a little late tonight, Alice."

"Yes, Grandmother. Miss Lucchesi was talking to me about fingering."

"Fingering is of the essence, of course," Irena smiled, "when you study the violin. Nevertheless, I worry about you as the days grow shorter. I do not like to think of you out there on the streets in the dark."

"No, Grandmother."

"Draw the curtains now, Alice. Let us tuck ourselves up in the light and warmth, and hide away from the night."

Alice thought of the young man who had walked home with her. Miss Lucchesi said he was one of her most promising pupils. Ben Ackworth. He must have gone by now. I hardly said a word, Alice thought. He was very polite but he must have been bored by me. I don't think I shall ever see him again.

As she moved the drapes (how old? as old as Grandmother? older perhaps?) across the window, Alice watched thin veils of dust rising from the folds and settling in new patterns on the velvet.

Ben looked at the yellow light coming from the downstairs windows until the curtains were drawn. Someone had gathered all the warmth and comfort into the room. Someone, Alice perhaps, had shut him out, along with the darkness and the rising wind.

"It's a new recipe. Orange and a touch of coriander, to give an unusual flavour to the lentils."

"It's lovely, Aunt Bella."

"Then why are you not eating it more enthusiastically?"

Alice laughed. "I was thinking about something else. I was miles away."

Louise said: "It often happens to me. You inherit that from me. I can be doing the most mundane of tasks, and quite suddenly I'm in another place, with different people."

"You have always," said Irena, "been imaginative, Louise. Of course, I'm an old lady now and sometimes, you know, the past seems more real to me than the present."

Alice smiled to herself. Her grandmother claimed that she could remember fleeing to Paris at the time of the Russian Revolution. She spoke quite often of snowy landscapes glimpsed through carriage windows and small hands curled up in a muff made of grey fur, even though she could not have been more than three at the time. Irena had a gift for memories.

"Why," said Alice softly, "haven't I got any friends?" The three women stared at her, amazed.

"But you have," her mother answered at last. "You have me, and Bella and your grandmother, and Miss Lucchesi, and I know Madame Rochard is very fond of you, and told me, the last time I saw her, that your French is much improved."

"I mean friends of my own age." Alice looked at them. They seemed shocked at the suggestion. They could find nothing to say.

"If I went to school, to an ordinary school," she began.

Irena said: "My dear, I think we have discussed this before. You are lucky enough to have Bella here to teach you, and your mother also, and as you know, I have undertaken to instruct you in history, since I am the one who has seen such

96

a lot of it, as it were face to face. Why do you need a school?''

''Because,'' Alice said, ''I would meet people of my own age.''

''Not, however, of your type,'' Irena sniffed. ''You are still young, Alice. That is what you never realize. In the fullness of time, we will afford, perhaps, to send you to a finishing school, or a conservatory to study music. That will be different. There, you will mix with other young ladies.''

''Yes, grandmother.'' Alice said nothing else at all. I feel, she thought, as though we are besieged here, as though this were a fortress, and the whole world outside were one enormous enemy, ready to slide through the gates and the thickets of rhododendron and into our front door if we leave it open even a little. We hardly go to the shops because almost everything is delivered. All our clothes are bought from a catalogue. Aunt Bella says that it's more economical to buy like that, but I know it's because she's afraid. They're all afraid, and of everything. Ask them and they'll say the world has gone mad. The television sits in the corner and leaks unsavoury glimpses of what's really happening on to the faded carpets, and they hate it. They're frightened. They see the crime and the violence and the misery, and they shake and tremble because they think it might happen to them. Sometimes they see things — people embracing, people dancing, people undressing — and they're terrified of it happening to me. I know. They are trying to guard me . . . but until I see for myself, how do I decide if I want to be protected? No one else lives like this. I haven't any real friends, but I can tell from Madame Rochard and Miss Lucchesi and the other girls whom I see coming and going from lessons. They don't even dress like me. They wear lipstick, and shoes with high heels, and they walk down the road bravely, as if they're not afraid of anything, as if the world is theirs, as if they haven't got mothers who seem to die a little every time they go out of the door.

Alice looked up. ''I may be a little late,'' she said, ''next week, after the violin class. I may not be home till seven o'clock.''

Louise froze with a dessert spoon half way to her mouth. Alice could see the fear in her eyes.

''Miss Lucchesi is having someone to come and talk to us. A friend of hers who plays in an orchestra. She has asked us all, if we can, to stay. It will be all right, won't it?''

Irena said: ''But how will you get home? It will be quite dark by then. Perhaps we should send a taxi?''

''Chloe's mother will bring me in the car. Chloe said it would be quite convenient. They don't live far from us, after all.''

''In that case, yes,'' Irena said. ''I see no reason why not. But no later than seven o'clock, please, Alice.''

''No, Grandmother, of course not.''

Lies. I've told lies, Alice thought, and trembled. Why did I do it? I can't unsay it now. Mother is frowning and her hand is shaking so that she can hardly eat her dessert, and I've done that. She will suffer in advance for a whole week. Chloe. They know her from the Christmas concert last year, we played a duet. I've not said more than two words to her since then, but they remember her mother (so charming, so ladylike, so rich) because they have placed her in a box in their heads marked ''suitable''. Why did I do it? Because of Ben.

Perhaps he won't be there next week. Perhaps I imagined it all. But he said, he said he wanted to talk to me, to get to know me. And he looked at me. Alice felt a blush creeping over her body. Nobody has ever looked at me like that. How will I tell him I don't have to be home till seven? What will we do in that hour? Where will we go? Maybe he won't be able to spare the time. He'll be busy, and I'll have to walk around for a whole hour on my own. If only I could see him before next week. Seven days, just for thinking about him. Just for wondering. Seven days in which Mother will fret and try to hide her pain. It isn't worth it, thought Alice. I'll tell them.

''I'll have to see that your blue dress is clean for next week,'' said Aunt Bella.

The blue dress. They were regarding this as a special

98

occasion.

"Thank you, Aunt Bella," Alice whispered. "May I leave the table now?" What have I done? she thought. What have I started?

Alice and her mother were walking in the garden after breakfast.

"We should pick something for you to draw," said Louise. "We could make a lovely still-life. I feel I have been neglecting your drawing lately." She turned to look at Alice over her shoulder. "Are you happy?"

"Yes, Mother, I'm happy."

"I love this garden," Louise said. (She doesn't really listen to me when I speak, thought Alice. Her mind flits about like a butterfly, settling on one thing, and flying off again at once.) "In the old days," she went on, "I hated it. It was too formal. But now that it is always slightly overgrown. Poor Bella does her best, of course, but still . . ."

"I like it too," said Alice. It was true. Whenever she walked in it, she imagined herself in a tapestry, a pale princess in a forest of thorns and roses, thick grass, starred with flowers, circled round by high walls of pink brick. An apple tree grew flat against the wall on one side, and in spring, when it blossomed, it was like a huge, lacy fan all spread out in a froth of flowers and leaves. Now, in November, the pink and blue and lavender puffs of the hydrangeas had turned brown, the roses had gone, and the apple tree spread its bare branches like the fingers of a skeleton. Only Aunt Bella's herb garden still seemed green.

"Don't you feel sad for Bella ever?" Louise asked.

"I don't know." (How, thought Alice, do we come to be discussing Bella?)

"She could have married, if she'd wanted to."

"Perhaps she didn't want to?"

Louise smiled. "She wanted to . . . oh yes, but unfortunately, the man she wanted was not . . . available."

"I don't understand."

99

"Married," Louise whispered. "She could have had any number of others, but no, only he would do."

"What happened?"

"What happened is what always happens. She suffered, of course."

Alice was silent. It was in her mind to say: did you not suffer, too? Louise, as though reading her thoughts, said: "Of course, I suffered too. But then, I have you, haven't I, Alice?"

"Yes, Mother," said Alice.

"It's cold," said Louise. "Let's go in now."

"But what about the plants for the still-life?"

"Still-life?" Louise frowned. "Did I mention a still-life? Why, I wonder? Oh, well." She drifted towards the french windows. "Pick something if you like."

Alice bit her lip. She was finding it harder and harder to keep up with her mother's thoughts.

"Hello. Remember me?"

Alice smiled. "Of course. You're Ben. But what are you doing here? I'm on my way to Miss Lucchesi's."

"I know. I knew when your lesson was and worked out when you'd have to leave the house, and I've been skulking around here, waiting for you. It seems the only time I can ever talk to you is on the way to violin lessons and on the way back."

Alice said nothing.

"Your house," Ben went on, "is like an enchanted castle. One day I'm going to chop my way through those rhododendrons and wake you from your hundred-year sleep, Sleeping Beauty."

Alice looked down at the pavement. She said: "I told them I wouldn't be back till seven o'clock tonight."

"You did? Oh, Alice, that's tremendous. That's really great. Did you do it so that you could be with me?"

She looked up at him and blushed. "Yes. Yes, I did. I don't know what came over me."

"There's a café that stays open — a Greek place, just

around the corner. I'll borrow my brother's Lambretta so that we can just sit for a whole hour and then I'll drive you home. Don't look like that. It's quite safe, and I'll park around the corner." He lowered his voice and whispered dramatically: "No one will ever know."

Alice laughed. "I've never been to a café."

"Look," said Ben softly, "I'm going to kiss you and wake you up, my little princess, and then you can begin to live. O.K?" He took her face in his hands and kissed her eyes and her mouth, swiftly, tenderly, and then it was over.

"I must go in for my lesson now," she said. She couldn't look at him. She ran up the path and knocked at the door, her whole body seized by such a trembling excitement that she thought perhaps she was going to faint. She turned as she went in, and saw him still standing by the gate, waving. How will I live for the next hour, she thought. How will I wait?

"You haven't been practising enough, Alice," Miss Lucchesi said. "It's not like you. Your fingers look as if they're made of jelly. Where's the precision gone? You're wobbling about all over the strings. Now try and concentrate. Again, please."

Miss Lucchesi's right, Alice thought. I do feel as if my hands have turned to jelly. Only another half hour. How will I look at him, after that kiss? She closed her eyes and tried to concentrate. Miss Lucchesi sighed.

"Perhaps you're sickening for something, child."

"Yes," said Alice. "I think perhaps I am."

"But why," asked Ben, "can't you tell them? Straight out. Why can't you just say: 'There's a bloke I've met and I'm bringing him home for tea on Tuesday.' "

Alice smiled. "You don't understand. It's because of what's happened to them, in their lives, with the men they've known. They don't want it to happen to me."

"But it won't. Don't they realize that they were unlucky, all three of them? It doesn't necessarily mean that you will be.''

''I know. It's my mother, really,'' Alice sighed. ''Aunt Bella and Grandmother would put a brave face on it, but my mother would be . . .'' she searched for a suitable word, ''wounded. As if I had stuck knives into her.''

Ben said nothing. Alice went on: ''It's grown worse as I've got older. When I was a little girl, there were quite a lot of other little girls who used to come and play, but now . . .''

''Now there's the danger of your meeting dreaded and contaminating members of the opposite sex.''

''That's right.'' Alice blushed. ''My mother thinks that I might fall in love.''

Ben looked into her eyes and she lowered them and turned her head away.

''So?'' he said. ''That's quite normal.''

''She loved my father, you see, and he was cruel to her. He drank himself to death. I think he used to — you know — hit her.''

''I'm sorry,'' Ben whispered.

''It's hard for her. She's not like the others. They're stronger. But she — if you could meet her, you'd see. She's fragile. She looks as if a wind could blow her away.'' Alice shook her head. ''I can't explain. All I know is, I can't tell her about you. Not now. Not yet.''

''Then I shall have to be satisfied with once a week at the Prego Café.''

''Oh, no,'' Alice looked shaken. ''I can't always stay out this late.''

''Can't I climb the wall into your garden? At night? Could you be there?''

''No, not in the winter. What excuse could I make for going out into the garden?''

''Alice,'' Ben was frowning. ''Alice, do you want to see me again? Do you?''

''Yes. Yes, I do.''

''Then how are we going to meet? Walking to and from Miss Lucchesi's isn't my idea of seeing you. Is there no other way? Nowhere else you can think of?"

Alice said: "I think I could tell Madame Rochard. She might help us."

"Who's Madame Rochard?"

"I go to her for French conversation once a week. But she's, well, she's kind, and I think I could tell her about you, and maybe she will think of something."

"Will you ask her? Will you let me know?"

"Yes." Alice looked at him. "And I could telephone you. If you give me the number."

"Really? Will you? Every night?"

"Whenever I can. When they're not listening."

"Please, Alice. Please promise me you'll phone."

"Whenever I can. I promise." She glanced at her watch. "I think we should go now."

"Yes, I suppose so," Ben pushed his chair aside and stood up. "Back at the stroke of seven or the Lambretta will turn into a pumpkin."

He took her hand and led her out of the café.

Alice's arms were around his waist as they rode home, her hands like two white birds sleeping on the soft leather of his jacket. Once, the wind blew her long, pale hair forwards over his shoulder and strands of it caught his face and stroked it, and he could smell the fragrance of her drifting through his body. She had walked into that café like someone landing on the moon, her eyes wide with wonder and alarm. For a long time, she had just stared: at the green hair of that girl in the corner, at Andy behind the counter, sweating over the charcoal grill in his dirty vest, smiling under his moustache. The fluorescent light had made her skin even whiter. In her blue dress with the big, lace collar, she must have looked as strange to the other customers as they did to her.

"Alice," he said as she began to walk away from him.

"Yes?"

"I'm quite serious, you know."

"I don't know what you mean."

103

"I mean this. I'm not going to lose you. That's all. I don't care if I have to break the wall or really hack my way through that bloody hedge, I'm going to do it. Do you want me to? Are you ready for that? Because if not, you'd better say so now and I'll go away and never bother you again. You have to be the one to say."

It burst from her lips before she could think, before she could stop it: "I couldn't bear never to see you again."

"You'll see me," he smiled. "I'll storm the battlements and carry you away over my saddle."

"I must go now," Alice said. "It's seven o'clock. Please let me go."

"Will you telephone later?"

"I'll try. Please. I'm going now. Goodbye."

"Kiss me goodbye."

"Here?"

"Why not?"

He put his arms around her, to hold her, but she struggled free.

"I can't . . . I feel as if . . . they're watching."

"Nonsense," Ben said. "The house is around the corner. I'm going to kiss you, and I don't care who sees us, so there."

Alice closed her eyes as his face came nearer. He kissed her gently and stroked her hair.

"Fly away now," he said. Alice ran without looking back, scarcely feeling the pavement beneath her feet.

"Hello, is that Ben? Yes, Grandmother and Aunt Bella are downstairs in the kitchen and my mother is playing the piano. No, I feel fine. What do you mean? I haven't thought better of it. My French lesson is on Tuesday. I'll ask. They thought I looked flushed. Ben, I must go. Someone'll come. What? Yes, I know. Thank you for taking me. I enjoyed it. Yes, you too. Sleep well. I'll see you."

Alice put the telephone down carefully, and looked at herself in the small, oval mirror hanging above it on the wall. There were too many mirrors in the house: long, thin ones in polished mahogany frames, round ones, oval ones, and the gigantic mirror up there in the dark studio. She had never really noticed them before. Tonight, wherever she looked she saw herself reflected and transformed, her face shining as though she had quite suddenly woken up after a long sleep, filled with lovely dreams.

Madame Rochard lit a cigarette and settled back, white-haired, soft and plump in a soft, plump, lavender-coloured chair packed with an assortment of tiny cushions covered in satin and velvet and petit point.

"Eh bien, ma petite," she said. "Now we stop the French. You have, as they say, something on the mind, no?"

"Yes," Alice admitted.

"Then tell me." She laughed. "You know me. I have been your grandmother's friend since before you were born."

"I don't know how to begin," Alice stammered.

"Then I begin for you. You are in love."

"How did you know?"

A rich chuckle started in Madame Rochard's stomach and gurgled up to her lips.

"My dear Alice, the symptoms of love are as clear as those of measles."

"But what can I do?"

"There is no cure, alas," said Madame Rochard. "Sometimes, it goes away all by itself, pouff, but sometimes," she paused, "sometimes not."

"But don't you see," Alice said. "I can't tell them. They don't know."

"Aah! That is the problem. I understand."

"I can never see him properly. I don't know what to do. He'll grow bored. He'll stop caring. He says he won't, but I know he will."

Madame Rochard leaned forward.

"I have a suggestion. Perhaps I ring up Irena and say you need more French? Two hours more a week? Friday and

Saturday evening, perhaps?''

''Really? Would you? Oh, Madame Rochard, I love you. Thank you.'' Alice jumped up from her chair and ran to kiss the old lady.

''I do this,'' Madame Rochard said later, ''but I have a warning for you. It cannot continue like this. You will have to tell them. As soon as you can. Otherwise, there is no future. Do you understand that?''

''Yes, I think so, but I'm frightened. My mother . . .''

''Louise, ah yes, but you cannot sacrifice yourself for her. And I think that it will not be as bad as you fear.''

''Oh, I hope so,'' said Alice. ''I hope you're right.''

''I am. You will see. You must think of yourself, of your young man. What is his name?''

''Ben. Ben Ackworth.''

''Eh, alors, when do you bring this Ben to see me?''

Alice hid her love like someone hiding a precious jewel under their dress. She sat in the yellow light of the antique lamps every evening, watching her mother crocheting endless squares for a bedspread that would never be finished. Aunt Bella sat at the table, poring over catalogues, surveying the accounts, calculating. Irena simply sat, quite often with her eyes closed. From time to time one of the women would speak, launch a few words like small puffs of smoke towards the moulded plaster flowers on the ceiling, and then fall silent again. Alice thought: what if I told them now? Told them everything? She shuddered. It would be like a strong wind tearing into the warmth, ripping the fabric of the old rugs, overturning the lamps, plucking loose all the hair so skilfully wound up into neat and careful buns, unravelling her mother's dainty stitches, unravelling her mother. Her mother would be — Alice couldn't think of a word to describe how Louise might be. How can I tell her? She will think she is losing me for ever. But she isn't, and surely if I tell her, then after a while she will see that it is all right and forgive me. I can't lie to them. I can't. Every time I go to meet Ben, I can feel the weight of her on top of me. Suffocating me. Ben says I shouldn't feel guilty, that we're doing nothing wrong, but lying is wrong and deceiving your mother is wrong, and feeling so happy and so loving with Ben is wrong. Alice shook her head.

"Is anything the matter, child?" Irena had opened her eyes.

"No, Grandmother."

"Will you play the piano for us, Louise?"

"Of course, Mama."

Louise played Debussy until Alice thought she would scream. She wished she could be sitting in the Prego Café, listening to the mind-pounding rhythms of the juke box.

"Alice, it's not enough. Really. Two hours a week. We've been going on like this for months. Tea with Madame Rochard sometimes, and walking to Miss Lucchesi's and back, and those two hours that go by like water flowing through a sieve. I can't stand it. I just resent all the time I'm not spending with you, can't you see that? I love you. And I want to know them, know your family, walk into your house as if it were my house. I want more, that's all."

"I know, Ben. I'll tell them. I will, really."

"Truly?"

"Yes. I won't be able to tell them that I've been seeing you since November, but I'll tell them."

"Oh, Alice," Ben swung her around. "Alice, listen. There's a dance at the College in two weeks. I didn't dare to ask you. A spring dance. Will you tell them that I want to take you?"

"Yes. Yes, I will. I don't know how I'll do it, but I will."

"You won't regret it, you know. I'll never hurt you."

"I know."

"Will you pour the coffee, please, Alice?" Irena sat back in her chair.

"In a moment. First, may I say something, please?"

107

"Of course, child. What is it?"

"I've been invited to a dance." Alice felt as though the words were stones, rolling out of her mouth, bruising the air around them. Louise looked dazed. Bella's mouth hung open.

"A dance?" Irena whispered, but the sound went echoing round the room. "Who has invited you to a dance?"

"It's a pupil of Miss Lucchesi's. Ben Ackworth is his name. He's her best pupil. Next year he's going to the Royal College of Music. He's . . ." Alice did not know how to describe him. "He's very nice. He says he would like to meet you all."

For a long moment, no one said anything. Then Bella asked: "Is the dance to be held at his house?"

"No," Alice smiled. Was this all? Was there going to be no objection, no earthquake, no disasters? She felt a slight sense of anti-climax. "At the College."

The women looked at one another. Tears filled Louise's eyes. Bella was frowning. Irena said: "I shall have to telephone Miss Lucchesi about this young man. And we shall all have to meet him of course." She sighed. "Louise, pull yourself together. This had to happen, as you know. Did you think you could, we could, keep her locked up here for ever? Look at her. Look how lovely she is, like a flower. She has attracted attention, like a rose, and like rose, someone has picked her."

Louise fled from the room.

"Shall I go to her?" asked Alice.

"No, leave her," said Irena. "Bella will go later. She will learn to accept it, as we all must." She stood up and looked round the room as though she were leaving it for the last time. "Everything," she announced as she left, "everything will be quite different now."

Alice and Bella were left alone. I should say something, thought Alice. Anything.

"It's all right, you know," Bella said. "It had to happen. We couldn't protect you for ever."

"Then you don't mind?"

Bella smiled. "Of course we mind. Ahead of you lies heartache and plenty of it, but what can we do? I am, we all are, powerless. If we thought we could prevent it, we were deluding ourselves.''

''It can't all be heartache, can it? There must be some good things.''

''Oh, yes,'' Bella smiled. ''Yes, there are, of course. It's precisely those things that make the pain so . . . never mind. I shall put all that out of my mind and concentrate on your dress.''

Alice hugged her aunt, who smiled weakly.

''What is he like, this Ben?'' she asked. ''Is he handsome?''

''Yes, and kind and clever. You'll see. You'll like him. Even Mother will like him. I'm sure she will.''

''Let us hope, child. Let us hope.'' She stood up.

''No one had any coffee after all,'' she said, picking up the heavy tray.

That night, Alice lay awake for a long time, listening to the noises of the old house, trying to hear if her mother was weeping. No sound at all came from Louise's room. Perhaps after all, thought Alice, she is asleep. As she closed her eyes, she wondered why she had not told them about Ben right from the beginning. It hadn't been as bad as she had feared. It was going to be fine. It was going to be lovely. All the time . . .

''Goodbye, Mother. Goodbye Aunt Bella, Grandmother,'' Alice kissed them. Ben stood waiting beside the door.

''I'll take good care of her,'' he said. ''We won't be back too late.''

The three women were silent as Alice went down the front steps, her white lace dress foaming around her legs as she walked. They watched as the taxi drove away.

''Shut the door,'' said Irena, ''and let us go and eat. We cannot stand here forever.''

"She's gone," said Louise.

"She'll be back soon," Bella smiled at her sister.

"Never," said Louise. "She'll never come back."

"Don't be foolish," Irena sighed. "You will see her in the morning."

"I know," said Louise, "but she will never come back — properly. Never belong only to us again. They," she waved her hand towards the door, "they will pull her away from here, take bits of her that used to be all ours, and she'll be like a visitor here."

"Are you happy?" Ben asked.

"Oh yes. Yes." And it was true. Alice turned her face to him and tried to erase from a corner of her mind an image of Louise standing like a ghost in the doorway of the house, watching her leave.

8. Tea in the Wendy House

We're very lucky. Everybody says so. Lucky to have parents who didn't throw up their hands in horror and carry on about unmarried mothers, being too young to know our own minds, etc.

"It's very lucky," said my mother, "that you love one another so much. After all, you've known him all your life. He's always been like a brother to you. Not exactly a whirlwind romance."

I said nothing, but my mother didn't seem to notice. She went on: "It's a pity you didn't wait a little longer, but there you are. Look on the bright side. You'll still have your best years left over when your children are grown-up."

"Are they the best years?" I asked. "I thought now was supposed to be the marvellous time, and we're all meant to be living it up, burning the candle at both ends, finding out what we want to do with our lives."

"Yes, well." My mother looked up from the sewing-machine. She was busy giving some final touches to The Dress. "That's true, of course, but I've always thought that youth was wasted on the young. Someone once said that. I can't remember who it was, but I've often thought how true it is. You've got a lot to be happy about. Graham's very good to you, and he's got a job, and of course there's the house. You really have struck gold there. Not so many young people start out with a place of their own. It needs a bit doing to it, I know, but it's yours. You work on it, and it'll be a showpiece in no time."

Showpiece. You wouldn't know just by looking at it. A

small, terrace house in a dingy street. No trees. No front garden, just two feet of concrete between the house and the pavement, with a little wall to separate us from the road. No back garden either. A tiny yard full of scrubby tufts of grass trying to look green, and someone's garage wall at the end. Beyond that, more terraces, and windows with grey curtains. It doesn't matter what colour they were to begin with. In this kind of house, in this kind of street, they soon collect a grey film that makes them all look much the same.

Still, my mother was right. We were lucky. Graham, articled to a solicitor well known in the town, with a steady future of respectability clearly written all over his face, had inspired the building society to uncharacteristic flights of generosity. And my parents, who, as Dad put it, ''have quite enough to see you right'' from the sale of used cars in Dad's showroom, had paid the deposit for us as a wedding present. And I? I had passed my A-levels very nicely, thank you, and perhaps one day, I might be able to make use of them and train to be a teacher when my own child was at school. That was what Mum said, anyway. Meanwhile, we had a house.

''You've no imagination,'' Graham said the other day, as we stood at the window of what was going to be the baby's room, and looked out at the muddy patch behind our house. ''I can fix a trellis to that garage wall, and we can have climbing plants all over it. Next year. And we can plant grass seed. We can have crazy paving, with those stone pots that have flowers poking out of holes. You know, sort of Spanish.''

A hacienda in Grafton Road? Perhaps I could wear a mantilla to hang nappies on the line? I didn't say anything, because Graham was so enthusiastic, but I couldn't see it. I was too preoccupied with what I felt: about the baby, about Graham, about *now* to be able to visualize the future. Also, in our house I still think of the woman who used to live there. We saw her once. When we looked at the place for the first time. She seemed very ordinary. But her kitchen wallpaper, from floor to ceiling, was a mad pattern of Dutch tiles, bright blue and white, with little Dutch children in clogs stomping about happily, and cows and windmills and tulips: the works. It made you dizzy to look at it. It wasn't very clean either, so the Delft blue was spotted with grease and damp, brown in some places, yellow in others.

''We'll have to get rid of all this,'' Graham had whispered then, and I had agreed.

We stripped the kitchen last week, and painted it. Now it's glossy cream and pale blue and beautiful, but I find myself looking out of the window at the broken slats of the fence between our house and the next, and understanding very well why canals and tulips and windmills and clear blue Dutch skies had been important to the woman who had stood in that kitchen before me.

The Wendy House is very pretty. The curtains at the tiny windows are spangled with yellow flowers. The wooden walls are painted yellow too, like butter, daffodils and the hearts of daisies. The table is white and there are four little white stools. Inside the Wendy House, everything is comforting and bright. Inside the Wendy House, even on the dullest day, everything is bright and pretty. Yellow and white.

''Let's try it on then,'' said my mother, and I stood up obediently with my hands above my head while she slid the silky material over my arms. ''There!'' she breathed. ''I think that's just right now, don't you?'' I looked in the mirror. Perhaps not the most beautiful bride in the world, but O.K. I would have been quite happy with something new from a shop, but no, I was to have a Proper Wedding Dress (even if it wasn't white) and a Proper Wedding, with all the trimmings. As my mother put it:

''There's no reason not to have a celebration, just because there's a baby on the way. Perhaps one should celebrate even more.'' I wasn't going to be cheated out of my Day to Remember, oh no, and neither was she.

This dress reminds me of my first long dress. I was fourteen, Graham was fifteen. There was a dance at the Church Hall. He asked me to go.

"I'm going to that thing on Saturday," he said, leaning against our coal bunker. "You know. At the Church Hall. Want to come?" He sounded as if he couldn't give a damn either way.

"O.K." I yawned, sounding as if I could take it or leave it.

"Seven-thirty, it starts," he said, "and ends at half-past eleven."

"Great." My heart was thumping. I wished he would go away so that I could go upstairs and look at all my clothes. Maybe I could have a new dress. Maybe Mum would make one. We'd walk into that Church Hall, and everyone would gasp. Graham, when he came to pick me up, would stand back and burst into song, like that man in "Gigi": "Why, you've been growing up before my very eyes!"

Mum made the dress. It was red and frilly, and I thought I looked terrific. Graham, when he saw me, looked me up and down and said: "You'll do." And it was wrong. Everyone else was wearing ordinary daytime clothes. They stared at me, but didn't say anything. I wanted to die. Graham, I thought, would hate me, and would never even take me fishing with him again, down on the Canal. Perhaps he wouldn't speak to me again. I danced, and went through all the motions of enjoying myself, but we left early and on the way home I burst into tears, and cried and cried and wouldn't stop. Graham said nothing. That made me furious. I wanted to hit him. We passed the tree stump that we used to play "King of the Castle" on, years ago.

"Lynn," Graham said. "Lynn, come and sit down."

I sat. I was exhausted. I'd stopped crying. I didn't have the strength to squeeze out one more tear. Graham knelt beside me, and took out his handkerchief. Without saying a word he wiped my face gently, holding my head steady with his other hand.

"I'm sorry," I whispered. "I wanted to look just right,

and I . . . it was dreadful.''

''I thought you looked,'' he hesitated, ''beautiful.''

I couldn't see properly in that light, but by the way he kept his head turned away, I could tell he was blushing. I loved him for saying that, for trying to cheer me up. I laughed.

''I looked dreadful,'' I said. ''Well, not dreadful, exactly. Just wrong.''

''I didn't think so.'' He sounded angry.

''I'm sorry, Gray. I know you were being kind.''

''I was bloody well *not* being kind,'' he yelled.

''Ssh! You'll wake everyone up.''

''I meant it,'' he whispered. ''I mean it.'' And he bent his head so that his mouth was hidden in the folds of my skirt, and said so softly that I could hardly hear it, but I felt it more than heard it, through the red material, murmured against my leg: ''I love you.''

I didn't know what to do. Suddenly Graham, whom I'd known all my life, was different. I didn't recognize him. I didn't recognize his voice, the way he was speaking. He looked up. His mouth was trembling. All at once, he got up. I thought: he's sorry now, he's sorry he said all that. He wants to go home. He wants everything to be like it was before. I stood up too. My legs felt shaky. Graham didn't move.

''Are we going home now?'' I asked in what I hoped was more or less a normal voice.

''In a minute. Lynn?''

''Yes.''

''Can I kiss you?''

I blushed. I could feel the redness spreading all over my face, down my neck, covering me. I didn't know what to say. He took my head between his hands carefully, gently, like someone holding a precious vase. I closed my eyes. He kissed my mouth, and it felt like warm butterflies brushing my lips, softly, quickly, and then it was gone.

We walked in silence. Not touching. When we reached home, we stood for a moment beside the tree near my gate.

''Thank you for a lovely evening,'' I said. ''I enjoyed it.''

"Rubbish," said Graham, "you hated every minute of it."

"Not every minute," I said, and then he took my hands and pulled me right up to him. I could feel the warmth of his body. This time when he kissed me, his mouth stayed on mine, and I opened my lips a little, and so did he, and I could taste him in my mouth.

"I reckon," he said, after a while, "that with a bit of practice, we could get quite good at this."

He was grinning. I could hardly walk up to the front door. "Hey," he whispered after me, "you look smashing."

I went to bed quickly, even though my mother was waiting to hear all the details. I stared into the mirror, expecting to see huge marks like red flowers blazing on my mouth where I had been kissed, but I looked just the same as I always did. Lying in bed, I thought of what Graham had said: "With a bit of practice." That meant he was going to kiss me again. And then again. And I wanted him to.

That was three and a half years ago. The kisses went on. They changed in character: grew as we grew older. And, of course, after we had become used to them, we wanted more. And different. New excitement. New pleasures. So one thing, as the saying goes, led to another.

Lynn and Mandy are playing in the Wendy House. They are having a tea party. There are teacups made of red plastic on the table, and a little teapot. Lynn and Mandy are Mummies. They have dolls. The dolls are babies. They are pouring pretend tea into the teacups. Drinking it. Pouring more tea. The dolls fall over. They are picked up again.

A boy comes into the Wendy House. He sits on one of the little white stools. He pushes a doll over. Grabs the teapot out of Lynn's hand. Lynn burst into tears.

"Go away! We don't want you!" she shrieks. A lady comes to see what the noise is all about. She understands at once.

116

"Graham! You mustn't do that. It's Lynn's and Mandy's teaparty. You mustn't spoil it. Go and play on the slide and let the girls get on with their game. They're much smaller than you. You're a big boy of four."

Graham is taken to the slide. He looks longingly at the teapot and the tiny red cups. Lynn and Mandy are passing round pretend cakes. The babies are being naughty. Lynn is shouting at her baby. "Naughty boy! Naughty!"

Inside the Wendy House, everything is bright and pretty.

There's nothing left in my room now. All my clothes are packed in suitcases, stacked in the bedroom of our little house, waiting to be put away. Every single childhood thing that I possess, all the dolls, books, cuddly toys, the posters of David Bowie and John Travolta, everything has been collected by my mother, and put into trunks in the cellar.

"Waste not, want not," she said cryptically. "You must think of your child."

What makes her think that my child will want posters of David Bowie and John Travolta, anyway? They'll be old hat by then. They're already old hat. A child. That's what I still am to my mother. She would never say so, and I probably wouldn't think such a thing if I weren't pregnant, but pregnant-me thinks: she's keeping something of me, something of the child I was, in those trunks down there, so as not to lose me entirely, so as not to lose my childhood completely.

When I first found out that I was pregnant, I tried to run away. I didn't really think at all, not about where I was going, nor about what I would do when I got there. I didn't take any money with me. I didn't pack anything. I just went as I was and got on the first train I could find. To Stoke-on-Trent. By the time I got there, I'd changed my mind. I phoned Graham at work. I was crying.

"Come and get me, Graham. I want to come home. Please come and get me. I haven't any money."

Graham didn't ask questions. He simply said: "Stay there. Stay in the buffet. I'll be there. I'll come in Dad's car. I'll ring your mother. I'll tell her something, or she'll worry. Wait for me."

"I'm waiting."

I drank three cups of vile, greyish coffee. They seemed to go on and on. Then Graham burst into the buffet, out of breath. He must have run all the way from the car park. He pushed his way through the tables to where I was sitting. He pulled me to my feet, and flung his arms around me and squeezed me as if he wanted to gather me right into himself, never let me go, and we stayed like that for a long time, not speaking, rocking to and fro. The other people all around us must have thought — I don't know what they must have thought.

"Let's get out of here," Graham said at last. "Come and sit in the car."

We walked in silence to where the car was waiting. As we sat down, Graham said: "Please don't ever run away again, Lynn. Do you promise?"

"O.K.," I said. "Don't you want to know why I did?"

"In a minute. I just want to say something first."

"O.K."

"I don't know how to say it. It sounds so bloody corny."

"Go on."

"Will you marry me?"

I started laughing, and the laughter grew and grew, and Graham laughed too.

"I told you it was corny," he said. "But will you? Will you marry me?"

"It looks as if I have to," I said.

"No you don't. But I wish you would."

"Stupid! I do have to. Well, not have to exactly, but I'm pregnant, so it's just as well you asked me."

Graham said nothing. The laughter disappeared quite suddenly, out of the air.

"Don't tell me," I said. "You've changed your mind. I

118

don't blame you. You really don't need to saddle yourself with a wife and baby at nineteen, you know. I can quite see where it would tie you down.''

''I'm bloody furious, if you must know,'' he muttered, with exactly the same look he used to give me years ago if I jogged his elbow while he was making aeroplane models, or walked through his game of marbles, scattering coloured glass balls in all directions.

I screamed at him: ''What gives you any right to be furious? You're the bloody father. Whose bright idea was it, anyway? Who wanted me so much that it hurt? Who was it told me all those things? All those LIES? Anyway, who needs you? I'll have this baby on my own, and you can go and get knotted, for all I care!''

He put his head in his hands. ''You don't understand, Lynn,'' he whispered. ''You didn't understand. I'm not cross about the baby. I love you.''

''You said you were furious.''

''I was. I am. But not about what you think. Not about that.''

''About what, then?''

''About you running away. Away from me. When you should have been . . . oh, I don't know, running to find me. Do you see?''

''I didn't know if you'd want me.''

''That's what makes me angry. That you didn't know that. Do you really think I didn't mean any of those things I said?''

''Well, I thought you did, at the time. But it could have been the white heat of passion, couldn't it? A madness produced by the nearness of my luscious body?''

Graham laughed. ''It could, I suppose. But it wasn't. I love you, and I'll tell you something else.''

''What's that?''

''I'm quite pleased that you're pregnant.''

''I don't know if I am.''

''You'll be a lovely mum.''

''Is that all? A lovely mum? I used to have ambitions.''

"Really?"

"Yes. Trapeze artist, deep-sea diver, high-powered business woman, inspiring teacher — you name it, I've wanted it. I want to sing at La Scala and dance at Sadlers Wells."

"I don't think anyone can do both, can they?"

"Don't be so damned literal. You know what I mean."

Graham smiled. "Yes, I know what you mean." He started the car.

"We're going home."

"What'll we tell them?"

"The truth."

"Oh Lord. Really?"

"Yes, really. And Lynn? I want you to know something. I asked you to marry me before I knew . . . about the baby, I mean. I've always wanted to marry you."

"Have you? Always?"

"Well, since I was about six."

"You never said."

"It just never came up before, that's all."

Lynn and Mandy are having tea in the Wendy House.

"I'm the Mummy," Lynn says, "and you're the little girl."

"I want to be the Daddy." Mandy's mouth puckers up. Maybe she will cry.

"Silly." Lynn is scornful. "Girls can't be Daddies. Boys are Daddies."

"We haven't got a boy."

"I'll get Graham." Lynn runs to the climbing frame. Graham is hanging upside down by his knees from the top bar.

"Graham," she shouts. "Come and play. Come and be a Daddy in the Wendy House."

"Don't want to."

"Come on." She tickles him under the arms and he hits her and climbs down. She pulls him over to the

120

Wendy House.

"I don't want to be a stupid Daddy in a stupid Wendy House."

"I've got cakes," says Lynn.

"Not real cakes."

"You can pretend they're real." She pushes him on to a stool. "You can pour out the tea if you like."

"I'm the baby," says Mandy.

"Can I put her to bed?" Graham askes Lynn.

"Yes." Lynn looks at Mandy. "Bedtime. Lie down over there."

Mandy lies on the floor. Graham covers her with a blanket. "Go to sleep, baby."

Lynn and Graham sit on white stools, sipping pretend tea out of the red plastic cups. The light pours through the sunshiny curtains, and glitters on the glossy, white paint of the table. Inside the Wendy House, everything is bright and pretty.

Lying in my bed, I think: this is the last time I shall sleep here. Every night for the next ten, twenty, forty, sixty years, I shall lie near Graham in the new double bed. My mother has slept in the same bed with my father for twenty-one years and shows no visible signs of distress, or even boredom. Will it be boring, ever? Like a comfy old cardigan that you wear because you're used to it? Perhaps one day I will feel like throwing the old cardigan in the cupboard, and long to wear something wicked: blood-red satin or black velvet. Will my daughter (because it will be a daughter) lie in her bed and think of me and Graham as I think about Mum and Dad? Did Mum think the same things about her mother? We are an endless chain of mothers and daughters, all fitting together like a set of Russian dolls stretching to infinity, and it makes me feel dizzy just to think about it.

Yesterday, we finished painting the front room of the house. We painted it white. The curtains were all ready to hang up. Mum had made them. The material, a lovely pattern of small yellow and white flowers, looked familiar to me, although I couldn't place it at first. I knew I wanted it as soon as I saw it. It stood out from all the other fabrics as if it were lit up.

My mother said: "With curtains like this, you'll think the sun is always shining."

Graham hung the curtains.

"Not bad," he said, lying back on the sofa to admire them.

"I think they're smashing," I said. "I think this whole room is going to look great."

"Come and sit down, Lynn. Come and try the sofa."

"It's no beauty."

"Beggars can't be choosers. We'll save up for a new one. At least it's comfortable."

I sat down and closed my eyes. I felt tired. All the time now I feel tired. It's the baby. Everyone says so. I felt warm, and tired and soft inside, all over.

"I'm very far away." I murmured. "I think someone is kissing me."

"You betcha," Graham whispered. "I'm kissing you. There is some doubt," he kissed my eyes and my lips and my throat and my hair lightly, gently, "that I will ever be able to stop."

"Don't ever stop kissing me. Don't ever, ever stop loving me."

"I never will," he said. "I never will."

"Graham," I said, tried to say, "Graham, we've got so much to do. Do you think we should? I mean, I feel strange here . . . please."

"It's me," he whispered, "remember? It's only me." And he kissed me, and touched me, and held me, and whispered love into my hair and my ears.

Later, Graham went out to get us some fish and chips. I lay on the sofa and looked at the curtains. Where had I seen curtains like this before? I couldn't think, but I felt strangely frightened, and longed for Graham to come back. Why? It was going to be a beautiful room, bright and full of sunshine.

It was going to be a lovely life, wasn't it? Wasn't it? I loved Graham. I wanted him. Didn't I? And my baby! I would love her. We would love her. The Dutch tiles had gone from the kitchen and I would sit at the new table and pour tea. I sat up then, just as Graham opened the door.

"Graham," I said, "I've just thought. Where I've seen curtains like that before."

"Well?"

"At our nursery school. Do you remember? We used to have tea in the Wendy House. The Wendy House had curtains a bit the same. Didn't it?"

"Can't remember, really. Here, take this off me."

We ate our fish and chips. Graham talked and talked, and I said very little.

Tomorrow, I'm moving in. Moving into my new home. Into my new life. Into the Wendy House. I should sleep. Beauty sleep. Can't look awful on my wedding day: "The bride wore pale pink silk jersey and purple circles under her eyes." The bride looked haggard — the bride — the girl — the child — Graham's lifelong friend — and life is very long, isn't it? Playmate, companion, partner, till death us do part, or do us part. Which? It doesn't matter, not really. Everything is arranged, all fixed up, painted. Bright and pretty.

There is no one in the Wendy House except Lynn. Mandy isn't there. Graham isn't there. A doll is sitting on one stool. Lynn pours tea into the red plastic cups from the small, red teapot. She picks the doll up and holds it on her lap. The sides of the Wendy House seem higher. Lynn can hear the other children talking, laughing, crying somewhere on the other side of the walls, but she cannot see them. She tries to open the small door, but it won't open. She pushes it and pushes it and the thin wood shakes, but no one comes to let her out. The walls of the Wendy House are covered in a pattern of Dutch tiles: blue windmills unmoving, children in clogs frozen like statues, unbending flowers

123

all in hard blue, and blue and white. Where has the yellow gone? Where are the white and yellow flowers at the window? Lynn rattles at the doorknob. Shouts. No one comes. No one answers her. She can hear them, talking, shouting, not at her. She cannot get out. She goes back and sits on one of the small stools, rocking the doll. The bright blue walls seem to be closing in around her, the ceiling is coming nearer and nearer. She is happy, rocking the doll. She is Mummy. Mummies love to rock dolls. Mummies love to play in the Wendy House. It doesn't matter that she can't get out. She pours another cup of pretend tea. Inside the Wendy House, even on the dullest day, everything is bright and pretty.